COVENANT

A Black Flagged novella
by
Steven Konkoly

Copyright Information

stevekonkoly@striblingmedia.com

ISBN: 978- 1717784001

Work by Steven Konkoly

The Zulu Virus Chronicles—Bioweapons/post-apocalyptic thrillers

"Something sinister has arrived in America's heartland. Within 24 hours, complete strangers, from different walks of life will be forced to join together to survive the living nightmare that has been unleashed."

Hot Zone (Book 1)
Kill Box (Book 2)
Fire Storm (Book 3)

Fractured State Series—Near-future black ops thriller

"2035. A sinister conspiracy unravels. A state on the verge of secession. A man on the run with his family."

Fractured State (Book 1)
Rogue State (Book 2)

Work by Steven Konkoly

The Perseid Collapse Series—Post-apocalyptic/dystopian thrillers

"2019. Six years after the Jakarta Pandemic, life is back to normal for Alex Fletcher and most Americans. Not for long."

The Jakarta Pandemic (Prequel)
The Perseid Collapse (Book 1)
Event Horizon (Book 2)
Point of Crisis (Book 3)
Dispatches (Book 4)

The Black Flagged Series—Black Ops/Political thrillers

"Daniel Petrovich, the most lethal operative created by the Department of Defense's Black Flag Program, protects a secret buried in the deepest vaults of the Pentagon. A secret that is about to unravel his life."

Black Flagged Alpha (Book 1)
Black Flagged Redux (Book 2)
Black Flagged Apex (Book 3)
Black Flagged Vektor (Book 4)
Black Flagged Omega (Book 5)

About COVENANT

A Black Flagged Thriller

COVENANT is a novella set in 2009, one year after the concluding events in *VEKTOR*, the fourth book in my Black Flagged series. The events in *COVENANT* serve as a bridge between *VEKTOR* and *OMEGA,* the fifth book. ***COVENANT* was previously published as *JET BLACK,*** in a fan-fiction collaboration that included a character from a different author's series.

Rights to this story have recently been returned to me, and I have republished the story as *COVENANT*, removing any crossover elements with the other author's series. Since I designed the story to flow seamlessly within the *BLACK FLAGGED* world, crossover was minimal and *COVENANT* represents the best of what *BLACK FLAGGED* readers have come to expect from the series.

I know you'll enjoy this novella length foray into the *BLACK FLAGGED* world. All of your favorite characters play a role in the story.

Happy Reading!

Steve

Character List

Avi – Mossad. Assistant strike team leader.

Karl Berg – Assistant deputy director, National Clandestine Service, CIA.

Richard Farrington – Black Flag, Russian Group leader.

Gilad – Mossad. Mission leader.

"Gosha" – Black Flag Russian Group sniper.

Timothy Graves – Black Flag electronic support team.

"Grisha" – Black Flag ground team leader.

Anish Gupta – Black Flag electronic support team.

Talia – Mossad operative. Strike team leader.

Alexei Kaparov – Deputy director, Bioweapons/Chemical Threat Assessment Division Federal, Russian Federal Security Services (FSB).

Character List

Enrique "Rico" Melendez – Black Flag sniper, trained by Daniel Petrovich.

Jeffrey Munoz – Black Flag operative. Latin America Group leader.

Daniel Petrovich – Black Flag operative, semiretired. Married to Jessica.

Jessica Petrovich – Black Flag operative, semiretired.

Yuri Prerovsky – Assistant deputy director, Organized Crime, Russian Federal Security Services (FSB).

Anatoly Reznikov – Former bioweapons scientist at Vektor Institute.

Brigadier General (retired) Terrence Sanderson – Black Flag leader.

"Yoshi" – Mossad sniper.

Valery Zuyev – Solntsevskaya Bratva, *Boyevik* (Warrior).

*To my family. Still the heart and soul
of my writing—and everything else.*

*I couldn't do this without their tireless support,
love and patience.*

COVENANT

PART ONE

BLACK EYE

Chapter 1

Talia pressed her lips together, spreading the burgundy shade of lipstick evenly. The dark red accentuated her tan skin, leaving just enough color to attract attention—or distract a bodyguard. She examined her appearance in the full-length mirror, searching for the smallest detail that might draw the wrong kind of attention. A missed button, frayed sleeve corner or errant wrinkle could spell disaster. The hotel staff dressed impeccably, one of the luxury resort's signature touches.

Finding nothing out of place on her tight-fitting outfit, she affixed a brushed silver, oval name tag just above the left breast pocket of her royal blue suit jacket. Today she was *Selena Amador, Senior Concierge, La Joya Azul Resort and Spa.* Tomorrow she could be a visiting European banker in Buenos Aires. Whatever they wanted her to be. She was their chameleon, and more often than not—their viper.

Talia turned from the mirror and approached the white-marble-topped, dark mahogany vanity next to the spacious sink, noting the watchful eye of the team's mission leader—and her stand-in husband for the operation. Without either of them saying a word, she removed a suppressed compact pistol from the top of the vanity and tucked it snugly into the custom holster sewn into her black leather Prada shoulder tote. A knockoff bag, she suspected. The Mossad's budget didn't include disposable thousand-dollar accessories—unless those accessories killed people. With the bag in place over her left shoulder, she smiled at Gilad.

"How do I look?" said Talia.

"Deadly as always," he replied, without expression. "I just hope deadly enough."

"I can handle two thugs at close distance," she said.

"If the guards are more alert than intelligence suggests—you walk away. It only takes the blink of an eye to pull a trigger. We'll find another way," he said.

"I just need to get within thirty feet," she said. "This ridiculous outfit will get me close enough."

"You're good, but not that good. You need to ensure two dead-center head shots. A skull ricochet might hit the door, alerting the guards inside. Fifteen feet minimum. Preferably five. The closer you get, the narrower their focus," he said.

Her concealed earpiece crackled. "Strike, this is overwatch. Shift change underway."

Gilad's eyes darted up and to the right momentarily, a subtle tell that he had received the same message.

"Five minutes," he said, glancing at his watch. "Let them settle in."

She nodded, slipping her hand into the shoulder tote and checking the holster action. Within a fraction of a second, Talia pointed the suppressed Glock 26 subcompact at her image in the mirror.

"Maybe twenty feet," said Gilad, finally smiling.

Chapter 2

Jessica Petrovich took a sip of cold sparkling water from a perspiring highball glass, setting it on the turquoise-painted, wrought-iron stand next to her chaise lounger. The vanishing ice cubes rattled and reorganized in the glass, reminding her to order another drink the next time she saw their server. Of course, if her observations proved correct, she'd probably never take a sip of the new drink. It didn't matter. She had to keep up appearances, and right now she played the role of a pampered wife, relaxing poolside with her husband—or the man pretending to be her husband.

Enrique Melendez, one of the few Black Flagged operatives she fully trusted, sat upright in the lounger next to the iron table, pretending to read a book. Behind his designer sunglasses, he scanned their wide view of the pool area, searching for possible threats and keeping an eye on their primary target. Her job was to watch their backs.

Their cover story as a fake couple was tight, but the Russians had plenty of money to throw around—and they didn't hesitate to back up their money with a healthy dose of intimidation. Her team's last minute arrival consisted of three expensive transactions outside of normal resort booking channels. Pricey to keep them discreet—she hoped. Of course, hope got you killed in this game.

She glanced over her shoulder again, feigning a search for their server. Noticing nothing out of place, Jessica's eyes darted to a balcony on the third floor. The expansive glass slider was fully open, thin white curtains waving lazily on the edges of the room's shadowy interior. Her husband, Daniel, was hidden in the room, carefully watching the team's target through binoculars. She wished he was next to her instead of Melendez, but Daniel had spent "quality" time with their target, and the team couldn't risk the possibility of recognition. Intelligence suggested that this might be their only chance to kill or capture Reznikov before he disappeared again.

"The Russians are on the move," said Melendez.

She eyed her gold, jewel-studded watch. "A little early."

Her earpiece filled with Daniel's hushed voice. "Shift change. Lots of movement in both suites. Time to head upstairs, my love. Munoz, you copy?"

"Lima Charlie. Ready to move," replied Jeffrey Munoz, who waited in a room on the target floor.

Munoz was one of the few surviving graduates from General Sanderson's first generation training program. Upon graduation from the Black Flagged program, Munoz spent the next few years infiltrating drug cartels in

Central America, while Daniel melted into the killing fields of the Balkan Peninsula. They never laid eyes on each other again until Sanderson rebooted the Black Flagged program several years later. Daniel trusted him, but she wasn't one hundred percent convinced. Munoz's loyalty ultimately landed at Sanderson's feet, a fact she couldn't reconcile.

"You should get out of the sun, honey," said Melendez. "It's probably not the best thing for you, given your condition."

"Still a comedian," she said, pushing herself up from a semi-reclined position. "I'll slowly work my way up to the room."

Jessica swung her legs over the side of the lounger and sat there for a moment, hands resting on the top of her swollen abdomen. Her one-piece, black bathing suit was stretched to the limit. She stood up slowly, shouldering a tan canvas beach tote.

"Be careful," said Melendez, lifting his glasses to look at her clearly pregnant stomach.

"Knock it off," she whispered.

"No. I actually mean it. Daniel, back me up here," said Melendez.

"Watch yourself, Jess," said Daniel through her earpiece. "The men guarding that suite would gut their own siblings for a paycheck. They won't hesitate to kill you, regardless of your *condition*."

"Well, shit, maybe I should give it one hundred percent, then. You know, based on this patronizing lecture," she said, picking up her canvas tote.

Melendez shook his head and mumbled, "Dude, it's been like this the whole trip."

"How do you think I feel? You're just the rent-a-husband," said Daniel.

"I heard that," said Jessica.

"You were supposed to hear that," said Daniel. "Make sure Munoz is ready before you hit the hallway security team. That's a tactically based recommendation, not a lecture."

"Yes, husband," she said, winking at Melendez.

"She's making fun of you," said Melendez. "I give up trying to read her."

"Join the club," said Daniel, quickly changing his tone. "The balconies are empty. Definitely shift change. I'll let you know when I can maximize the damage against the off-going security team."

"I'm on the move," she said, strolling toward the hotel lobby.

Chapter 3

Daniel Petrovich cracked a thin smile behind the 6X ACOG/RMR combination scope attached to his suppressed SOCOM 16 rifle. He loved that woman; no matter how much shit she gave him. The smile quickly faded with the thought of the task in front of her. He wished there was another way to ensure Reznikov's death, but short of detonating a bomb powerful enough to level a significant portion of the hotel, sending Jessica and Munoz into the suite appeared to be the only way.

He'd spent nearly every second that Reznikov had been awake during the past three days watching the balcony and praying that the Russian would make a mistake. All he needed was a clear line of fire for a few seconds. The suite's poolside-facing balcony sat three hundred and twenty-three feet away from his position. A head shot he could take with one hundred percent confidence and lethality—if the drunken shithead ever left the darkened confines of his suite.

In three days, Daniel had counted two possible opportunities, each carrying unacceptable risks. Two days ago, a few minutes before sunset, Reznikov ventured into the Jacuzzi on the north-facing side of the balcony, but a slatted privacy screen obscured his view of the Russian's head. Through the scope, he could see part of his target's body, but not enough to guarantee a head shot through the screen.

The second chance came yesterday afternoon, when Reznikov's scarred face materialized in the darkness behind one of the open balcony sliders. There one second—gone the next. He didn't have enough time to press the trigger after bringing the scope's illuminated red crosshair reticle onto the man's ugly visage. All he had needed was another second, and Jessica wouldn't be walking into a gunfight. They'd be back in their private beach bungalow on Anguilla, sipping cold drinks and enjoying each other's company.

In retrospect, he wasn't sure why they had agreed to take this mission. Attachment to the past? A sense of duty? Sanderson's snake-oil charm? Probably all of the above. Not to mention that they both missed the work—a very unhealthy addiction in their area of expertise. There was no point reflecting on another bad choice. All of his mental energy needed to stay focused on the two hotel suites. The better his shooting, the better his wife's odds of surviving the assault. That was his only purpose right now. His only mission.

He released the trigger safety and scanned the balcony adjacent to Reznikov's suite, waiting patiently for the off-going crew. Shirtless, they would quickly settle around the table, swigging vodka out of bottles and furiously puffing cigarettes—trying to make up for the reduced nicotine and alcohol intake incurred during their overnight watch.

Members of the on-duty team were occasionally allowed onto the main suite's balcony to get a nicotine fix—but it wasn't enough. Not based on the chain-smoking that occurred before and after a shift. The scene was almost comical. They'd drink and smoke until they nearly passed out in their chairs. One by one, they'd haul their pasty, tattooed bodies back into the suite to sleep for several hours. Today, Daniel would expedite the balcony-clearing process. He'd kill or disable every guard visible on the terrace, leaving the rest to Munoz. Then he'd shift his deadly eye to Reznikov's suite, searching for targets of opportunity.

Chapter 4

A fragrant breeze enveloped Jessica at the edge of the lobby, the sweet scent of native blue crown flowers filling the spacious open-air lobby. She avoided eye contact as she picked up the pace, heading straight for the elevators that serviced the northern wing of the hotel. Once inside the brass and mirror elevator car, she pressed the number four and examined her reflection.

The halter dress swimsuit accentuated her toned arms and shoulders, while the deep V-neckline highlighted the results of the suit's patented push-up technology. Of course, no amount of maternity-wear tricks could draw the observer's eye away from the main event—her obviously pregnant stomach. Just as well. She only needed one of her physical features to catch their attention.

The door opened, emptying into a spacious, white marble elevator lobby outfitted with turquoise cushioned rattan furniture. Floor-to-ceiling windows opened to the gardens and pool between the two hotel wings. Somewhere in the sea of tan pool umbrellas sat Melendez.

The bright vestibule connected to a wide hallway that

ran the length of the fourth floor. She took a few deep breaths and stepped into the passageway, turning right. At the far end of the hallway, a set of windowed doors requiring a room key led to a separate luxury suite hallway. Through the doors, she caught a distant glimpse of the men guarding Reznikov's suite—nothing but pastel-colored shirts at this point.

Jessica walked briskly toward the luxury suite area, her eyes darting briefly to the right as she passed room 425. Jeffrey Munoz lurked behind that door, no doubt watching her pass. She would call him forward once the guards had been eliminated. Munoz would breach the room adjacent to Reznikov's suite, quickly dispatching the guards inside while she wreaked havoc on the Russian scientist. Once Munoz was finished, he'd join her in the festivities—not that she'd need the help. With Daniel targeting the guards visible from his sniper's perch, the Russians would never know what hit them.

She inserted her room key and opened the door, drawing the immediate attention of the two stocky men seated in rattan chairs taken from the off-duty guard suite. Every second of every day in the hallway had been recorded and reviewed by her team. As predicted, the same two guards started the day shift. For the past three days, the Russians never changed the guard schedule, which made her job easier. She'd interacted with all of the guard teams by this point, assessing their state of readiness, and most importantly—their potential state of distraction. The two men standing in front of her represented the far ends of the spectrum.

The goateed brute wearing thick gold chains under his half-unbuttoned light blue, short-sleeved shirt eased his left hand behind his hip. He was the least distracted of the guards she'd seen, but he was the most obvious about his intentions. Broadcasting the firearm behind his back, along with his apparent eagerness to use it, earned him the dubious honor of dying first.

The second man, standing three inches taller and many pounds heavier than "goatee," crossed his arms and grinned at her—before slowly moving his dead eyes down her body. He was second in line to die, but would leave this world in a far more painful, dramatic fashion. She'd seen what men like this were capable of, and took pleasure in erasing their legacy.

She smiled and nodded demurely, fiddling with the ends of her long brown hair as she disappeared into the suite. Once inside, the coy demeanor vanished—eclipsed by the practical, efficient operative at the core of Jessica's existence. She stepped out of her strappy sandals and quickly replaced them with black, low ankle cross-training shoes. Not exactly a match with her swimsuit, but she had yet to see any of the guards look at her feet. A quick trip to the safe located in the suite's master bedroom yielded a loaded semiautomatic compact pistol, a nylon belt fitted with five magazine pouches and a five-inch suppressor.

Jessica dropped the belt in her canvas tote, which she switched to her left shoulder, and screwed the suppressor onto the barrel while she walked to the front door. She placed her pistol on the beige marble-topped foyer table, next to an open laptop. The laptop display showed three images provided by a sophisticated, wireless camera drilled into the door's peephole. The leftmost image focused on the entrance to Reznikov's suite; the middle image gave her a traditional peephole view of the hallway surrounding her door and the rightmost image centered on the entrance to the suite area. Two private stairways flanked the windowed door beyond the suites, leading to the pool or beach.

She studied the guards, waiting for them to settle back into the comfortable seats they would die in. When "goatee" was firmly planted in his chair, Jessica gripped the pistol in her right hand and slid it behind her thigh. She'd drill the first guard through the forehead, then target the bigger man's neck. The thought of him grasping at the wound, struggling to breathe made her happy. Imagining a serrated blade cutting deep into his stomach caused a devilish grin. If she did this right, there would be time for both. Of course, if she missed his neck on the first shot, she'd take him down instantly with a head shot. She couldn't risk him raising the alarm.

"I'm in place, ready to take out the guards," she whispered.

"Backup ready," stated Munoz.

"Poolside ready," reported Melendez.

"ES ready. Surveillance camera outside of the target suite entrance has been placed in an endless loop. Hotel security and communications systems are disabled," announced Timothy Graves, the team's electronic support (ES) technician.

Stationed on board one of the yachts in the resort's

nearby marina, Graves and Anish Gupta, the team's hacker, had used the boat's sophisticated communications array to access the hotel's servers. "Child's play," he had reported to the team. Coopting the wireless signal from the Russian-installed camera had proven more difficult. Remotely accessing the laptop next to her on the table, he systematically attacked every wireless signal in range, decrypting every signal within seconds, except for one. GHT81432D1 required a brute-force software program.

"Copy," answered Daniel. "Monitor local emergency response and police frequencies. Lots of cell phones around."

"Monitoring," said Graves. "I can delay their arrival if the need arises."

"Let's hope it doesn't," said Daniel. "Jess, the show is yours. I start shooting once you breach the door."

"I'm walking out of the—hold on," she said, her peripheral vision catching movement on the computer screen.

The guards were out of their seats, standing in the same menacing poses they assumed every time she passed through the secure doors at the end of the hallway. A quick glance at the rightmost screen showed a woman dressed in a royal blue jacket and khaki slacks stepping through the door.

"Looks like a member of the hotel staff decided to pay our friends a visit," said Jessica.

"How often has that happened?" said Munoz.

"Once," replied Graves, "and the Russians raised hell."

"Maybe they forgot to pay a bill," said Daniel. "Is she alone?"

"As far as I can tell. The hallway beyond the doors looks empty," said Jessica. "I see a hotel name tag."

"Maybe she's room service," said Melendez.

"She's not carrying anything besides a tote bag," said Jessica.

"I meant *she's* the room service," he replied.

"I know what you meant," she said.

"Let's see what happens," interrupted Daniel. "If she goes away and the guards ease back into their seats, we'll execute the plan. If not, we wait another day. Watch this one closely."

"Got it. She's passing my door," said Jessica.

Chapter 5

Talia walked past the door leading to the off-duty guard suite and approached the two men standing in front of the target suite's double entrance. Without breaking eye contact with the smaller guard, she noticed his left hand drifting slowly along his hip, most likely headed to a concealed holster. His larger compatriot crossed his arms and just stared at her chest. Easy pickings if she timed it right. When she reached the last door in the hallway, the first guard's hand moved past the point of no return, disappearing behind his hip.

She smiled warmly even as her right hand slipped into the tote and effortlessly yanked the pistol from the internal holster. Her pistol cleared the bag before his expression changed. The first suppressed bullet hit him square in the face, spraying the suite's white doors with a mosaic of deep scarlet pieces. The second bullet hit the gawker between the eyes, finishing the gory masterpiece behind them. The man's lustful expression remained intact as he collapsed against the side of the hallway, arms still folded uselessly in front of him.

"Both guards down. Move up," said Talia.

***

"Shit," whispered Jessica, watching the second guard crumple. "The hotel bitch just shot the guards."

"Say again!" hissed Daniel.

Jessica studied the screen for a moment. The impeccably dressed woman paused momentarily in a two-handed firing position before lowering her pistol and continuing toward Reznikov's suite. She was good, but walking up to two men in a hallway and shooting them dead wasn't exactly the pièce de résistance of black ops fieldwork. Movement in the rightmost screen drew her attention away from the shooter. Two men shouldering suppressed submachine guns entered the hallway through one of the private access stairwells inside the suite area.

"Two additional shooters entered the hallway," she said.

"Abort mission. Let them finish the job," said Daniel.

"They approached the guards without disabling the camera. How professional can they be?" she said, placing her hand on the doorknob.

"She's right," said Graves. "I've detected no electronic attempts to override the Russians' security system."

"Stand down!" said Daniel.

"We only get one shot at this guy," she said. "They won't shoot a pregnant woman."

"Are you out of your mind!" she heard, before jamming the pistol into the canvas bag.

***

Talia pivoted left and assumed a combat shooting stance when she heard the door open. She aligned the pistol's tritium sights with a dark-haired woman's head and applied pressure to the trigger. The woman screamed and backpedaled into the door frame, giving Talia a moment to assess the situation. Her eyes scanned the woman, immediately noticing that she was pregnant. Shit. The last thing she wanted to do was endanger this woman.

"Go back in your room," Talia commanded.

The woman pressed an index finger against her lips and shook her head. She looked terrified.

"There's two more inside," the woman whispered in Spanish, crossing the doorway to approach her. "They just passed out. I need help."

Talia took a step backward, extending an open hand to stop Gilad and Seth from coming any closer. The woman kept her hands in the air and slid against the wall—afraid to look at her pistol. What the hell was going on in there? A rage ignited at the thought of these Russian pigs violating this woman. She shifted the semiautomatic to the open doorway and reached out to the frightened woman.

"Two targets in room. Passed out," she whispered to her team, turning her head to give the woman instructions that might keep her alive.

An unexpected surge of pain shot up her right arm, forcing her to drop the pistol. Before she could react, the woman had slipped behind her and locked a forearm across her throat, pressing the edge of a knife under her right jawline. Repeated shots from a suppressed pistol next to her head tore into the two Mossad operatives. They died without firing a shot—their line of fire obstructed by an operative careless enough to become a human shield.

***

Jessica pressed the trigger three times in rapid succession, the bullets stitching high across the second assassin's chest and knocking him to the blood-splattered marble floor. With the two threats eliminated, she no longer needed a human shield. She twisted the gun and placed it against the woman's head. What happened next didn't make sense. The woman's head slipped under her arm as she fired the pistol, the 9mm steel-jacketed bullet hitting the wall next to them. She barely registered the fact that the pistol's slide had locked back before her own knife came back at her.

The elbow shot to her knife-wielding arm knocked the razor-sharp blade into her right shoulder, slashing bare skin. The woman in front of her twisted, facing her long enough to grip the same arm and torque the elbow outward and down. She knew exactly what was coming next, but had no way to stop it. With Jessica's arm yanked downward, the assassin jabbed the short knife into her stomach. A sharp pain creased her abdomen, and she let go of the knife—her only defense against a repeated stabbing with her own blade.

With the knife gone, the assassin tried to force her arm into a permanent hold, but Jessica lashed out with her empty pistol in her disengaged hand, connecting with the side of the woman's head. They both stumbled back a few feet before scrambling after the weapons on the floor.

Jessica didn't have to look far. The killer's still-loaded pistol lay on the floor between them, beckoning her to try to grab it. In the fraction of a second it took her to process the situation, the woman flicked open a serrated blade and lunged.

Desperate to keep the pistol out of play, she stepped into the attack, blocking the underhand stab with a forearm and simultaneously striking the woman's face with the empty handgun. The impact gave her the moment she needed to step on the pistol and slide it behind her, temporarily removing it from the equation.

She heard it skim along the smooth marble floor and hit a wall. She hoped it was a wall. If it somehow got past the guards and hit the suite's entrance doors, they were screwed. The door had a peephole.

Chapter 6

He shook his head at the image in the mirror, barely able to stand his own face. The deep, mottled scar running from mouth to ear along his left cheek hadn't improved. His captors made sure of that. Sorry—liberators—though the distinction ran a bit murky from Reznikov's perspective. His "liberation" involved being smuggled into a third world shithole stuffed inside the dirtiest freighter possible, then shuffled from one fetid jungle hideout in South America to the next.

Occasionally, they occupied a marginally suitable structure near a town that smelled little better than a highway truck stop bathroom. Not that he really noticed the stench over his rotting feet and perpetual body odor. He sweated incessantly in the jungle, even when he was fairly certain that his body had already expelled all fluids save for the very blood coursing through his veins. The "dry sweat," as he called it, produced an odor that would repulse even the most deodorant-intolerant Muscovite.

At least they hadn't deprived him of vodka. They knew better. Without his daily ration, he would have killed himself trying to escape—and that wouldn't go over well with the big man in Moscow. He had them over a barrel in that regard. Their whole purpose in life was to keep him alive so he could one day return to make their *pakhan* money. Incredible sums of money, from what he guessed. There was a method to this madness, though it was hard to discern when your own body odor kept you awake at night, along with the unbearable heat and the constant fear of a thumb-sized bug crawling over your face.

His exile to the jungle served two purposes, both "in his best interest," he was told. He'd hate to see what wasn't in his best interest. Primarily, the Solntsevskaya Bratva used their shadowy network of South American drug contacts and human-trafficking farmers to *disappear* him. Admittedly, this made sense, though he would have preferred to vanish at a private beach house in Thailand. Of course, in an environment ripe with easy women and free-flowing liquor, he wouldn't be able to "focus" on his work, the real reason the Bratva kept him hidden.

A sophisticated Satcom rig and powerful computer suite accompanied them everywhere, allowing him to finish preliminary work and projections on his next masterpiece. They even cleared trees with explosives to create a line of sight to the nearest encrypted satellite on his behalf. Little did they know that he was recreating a virus he had long ago brought to virtual life in a sophisticated computer simulator. Nobody knew about this special research project. Not even the snoops at the Vektor Institute—sort of.

The only person that had ever heard him babble about

his prized creation was Arkady Belyakov, fellow bioweapons scientist turned snitch. They had both been drunk out of their minds at a dingy bar on the outskirts of Novosibirsk, when one too many shots of vodka sufficiently loosened Reznikov's tongue. Not an easy feat. He'd considered hitting Arkady over the head and pushing him off one of the small bridges on their walk back to the scientist housing area, but correctly reasoned that he'd be the prime murder suspect. They'd been the only patrons at the bar.

Instead, he walked arm in arm with Arkady, delivering him safely home to his family—all the time worrying if he'd said too much in the bar. Fortune smiled on him a week later, when Arkady's wife scolded him in the Vektor parking lot. Arkady had blacked out at home, skipping their planned family picnic the next day with a vicious hangover. Poor Arkady. The Americans executed him during their raid against Vektor Institute, at Reznikov's suggestion.

The thought of Vektor Institute's demise gave him a rare smile. Berg had done all of his dirty work, destroying Vektor's bioweapons laboratory and assassinating the cadre of scientists assigned to the program—eliminating any future competition. As Vektor Institute's only surviving bioweapons engineer, his market value rose considerably. Unfortunately, the only customers capable of freeing him from CIA captivity turned out to be the Solntsevskaya Bratva—an ironic twist of fate. He traded nearly all of his market value away for the simple pleasure of exchanging one captor for another.

He couldn't complain too much. His exile to the rain forest slums of South America was a small price to pay to be alive. Karl Berg had been moments from putting a bullet in his head—essentially winning the game of double crosses that Reznikov held so close to his heart. Only the Bratva's impatient quest to secure an invaluable asset saved him from an unceremonious death in the unremarkable woods of Vermont. He gently touched the scar—Berg would pay dearly for this, and his yearlong imprisonment with these cretins.

"Anatoly! Open the damn door," he heard, the doorknob rattling.

He'd kill them too when the time was right. They showed him no respect, treating him like shit all day long. Anatoly Reznikov was better than them. Better than all of this.

"You better not be passed out in there, you drunken piece of shit! We got a problem," said Valery Zuyev, his "handler."

Zuyev was closely connected to Matvey Penkin, a brigadier in the Bratva. Penkin was in the top tier of Solntsevskaya leadership, his position solidified by the income-earning potential of selling Reznikov's products to the highest bidder. The booze and women flowed freely when Zuyev visited, so he came to appreciate the man on a Pavlovian level.

"I'm taking a dump," said Reznikov. "Do you mind?"

"Cut the bullshit. I can hear your voice near the sink," said Zuyev. "We have a situation."

"All right!" he barked, downing the lukewarm vodka

in a thick tumbler and opening the door.

"There's always a goddamn situation with you," hissed Reznikov. "What now?"

"Something hit the door," said Zuyev, pulling him by the arm toward the front of the suite.

"Check the cameras, for shit's sake," said Reznikov, reaching for one of the half-full, open bottles of clear liquor on the nearest table.

"We've done that," said Zuyev, nodding at a computer station with a picture of the hallway.

The scene looked normal. Two guards seated several feet from the door.

"Then take a look through the peephole," said Reznikov, shaking his head.

"No shit," said Zuyev, yanking him around the corner leading directly to the entrance "We're taking precautions."

Taking precautions was an understatement. Six of the eight Bratva security guards crouched in various concealed locations, aiming black, short-barreled AKS-74Us at the double entrance. The two remaining guards kneeled behind furniture, facing the floor-to-ceiling glass that surrounded the suite.

"Shut the curtains and stay clear of the windows!" ordered Zuyev, spurring the two men into action.

While they closed the curtains, Zuyev settled in behind Reznikov's chief of security, a surly brute called Yergei.

"What are we looking at?" said Zuyev.

"Checking now," said Yergei, signaling for one of the guards to approach the door.

A muscular, tattoo-covered Russian crept to the door, slowly raising his head to the level of the peephole. He stared for a few seconds, then looked toward Yergei and shook his head.

"What are you seeing?" insisted Zuyev.

The guard crouched and moved quietly toward them, whispering when he arrived. "I see two women facing each other in the hallway. No sign of Misha or Yakov. Chairs are empty. I can't see the floor through the peephole."

Zuyev yanked him back into the living room area, stopping at the computer screen. The image clearly showed the two guards sitting in the chairs. They rubbed their faces and shifted in their seats—nothing seemed out of place. Reznikov suddenly felt nauseous. Berg's people had found him. The psychopath that had restarted his heart to torture him over and over again was here. It was the only explanation.

"The feed has been hacked," Reznikov squeaked.

"Indeed," said Zuyev, raising a small handheld radio.

"Victor One is under attack. Victor Two, I want you in the hallway immediately. Kill anyone you find," he said, waiting far too long for a reply.

"Victor Two, this is Zuyev. Answer your damn radios," he said, shaking his head.

"These people are good," whimpered Reznikov.

"Which people?" said Zuyev.

"They don't play by the rules. We're dead," said Reznikov.

Yergei tried to raise communications with the other

room, receiving no reply.

"Comms are hacked, or the team is already neutralized," said Zuyev, smashing his radio against the wall.

Reznikov stared at the pieces of the plastic radio scattered along the floor. They were most certainly dead. Well, not all of them. Berg had a surprise waiting for him. He was sure of it. The vodka bottles back in the suite tugged at him. Drinking himself to death sounded like the proper way to go. His gaze shifted to Zuyev, who spoke into a cell phone.

"Victor mainland, I want a marina extract immediately—with helicopter support. Do not use the encrypted radios. They've been compromised," he said, a garbled voice responding.

Zuyev patted his shoulder with a worried smile. "Looks like you're finally getting that boat ride you wanted."

"Wonderful," replied Reznikov, looking over his shoulder in the direction of the vodka.

Chapter 7

The catlike assassin wiped the blood off her right temple with a hand, fixing her with a murderous stare. Jessica considered reaching for the knife on the floor, but decided against compromising her stance. Instead, she pressed against the right side of her bulging stomach and slid her hand into a snug nylon-lined pouch inside the gel "pregnancy" insert. In a flash, she withdrew a retractable, serrated blade, flicking it open with one hand. The knife was smaller than she preferred, but equally lethal in her hands.

She was thankful that Daniel had insisted on the larger, seven-month belly insert. The knife turned against her had barely punctured the skin of her abdomen thanks to the massive, weighted bulge. A lucky break. The woman advanced, shaking her head in disgust at her choice of disguise.

"I'm going to make this hurt," the woman said in Spanish.

"But you killed my baby," said Jessica in English, pouting her lips and winking.

A bewildered look passed across the assassin's face. "Who the hell are you?"

"The competition," said Jessica, feinting a poorly aimed thrust.

The woman refused her bait, instead opting for another painful reminder that neither of them would escape the encounter unscathed. She slashed Jessica's forearm and retreated a step. Jessica winced.

"Not exactly a fair fight," said the woman, wiping a thin sheen of Jessica's blood on the arm of her jacket.

"Who said anything about a fair fight?" said Jessica, nodding behind her. "I wouldn't make any sudden movements."

Munoz had accessed the hallway, staying at the far end while pointing a suppressed MP7 submachine gun at the woman. Jessica stepped to the left to avoid getting hit by any bullets passing through the assassin. She was moments away from ordering the woman's execution when she received a disturbing question from Daniel.

"Are you breaching the room?" he said.

"Negative. Still dealing with the situation outside," she said.

"Shit. Something is wrong. I have unusual activity in the main suite. Guards are congregating toward the entrance. The off-duty suite still looks normal—wait, I'm seeing movement on the balcony. Engaging."

"Copy. Adapting to the change," said Jessica.

"Negative. Abort the mission," insisted Daniel. "We've lost the element of surprise. Get into the poolside stairwell with Munoz and melt away."

An insane idea hit her. Something about the assassin and her team suggested a level of skill and sophistication not typically seen with contract murder squads. The two men chose to die rather than open fire and risk hitting the woman.

"Who do you work for?" said Jessica.

The woman shook her head slowly.

"Both rooms have been alerted to our presence. Who is your target?" said Jessica.

"Who's your target?" said the woman.

"My orders are to kill or capture Dr. Anatoly Reznikov," said Jessica. "CIA orders."

The woman cocked her head and squinted. "Who the hell is Reznikov?"

"A bioweapons scientist working for the Solntsevskaya Bratva," said Jessica.

Screams erupted from the room behind and to the left of the woman. Daniel had started firing. Munoz crouched and shifted his aim to the door.

"We're running out of time," said Jessica. "Who is your target?"

She hesitated as the screams and crashes grew louder in the room.

"Valery Zuyev, a high-level—" said the woman.

"Zuyev?" interrupted Jessica. "He's just a seller for Reznikov's products."

"He's courting some dangerous clients with those products," said the woman.

"The Bratva can replace Zuyev," said Jessica. "Without Reznikov, they have nothing to sell."

"They we kill Reznikov," said the woman.

"Jess, you need to figure out what we're doing with her right away," said Munoz, shifting his knees and leaning into his weapon's stock.

Before she could answer, the off-duty guard suite's door flew open, and the hallway exploded.

Chapter 8

Talia crouched as the Hispanic operative with the suppressed MP7 dropped the first Russian to pass through the doorway with a perfect headshot, spraying the armed men behind him with an aerosolized red mist. The second man froze, his freshly decorated pinkish red face struggling to register what just happened. His confusion was short lived. A short burst from the operative struck him in the face and neck, whipping him sideways and exposing a man with a tattooed neck. The man fired his compact assault rifle on full automatic, splintering the doorframe from the inside and filling the hallway with bullets.

Talia sprang for the open suite door behind her, colliding with the bitch that had killed her team. The impact knocked them to the floor, and she momentarily considered stabbing the supposed CIA operative in the throat. Her survival instinct countered the temptation. They'd have to work together to get out of this alive, plus the woman had somehow managed to grab the empty pistol from the floor and reload it. The pistol was their only effective weapon at this point. She hoped they had more stashed in the room.

"We need more firepower," said Talia.

"This is it," said the woman, pushing her into the room and taking a covered firing stance at the door. "Unless you want to head back into the hallway."

A torrent of bullets tore into the doorframe, forcing the operative to move deeper into the room. She quickly switched sides and crouched, leaning out to fire several rapid shots at the Russians. A gurgled scream pierced the hallway, and the woman changed sides again, aiming the pistol carefully.

"I don't recommend it," said the woman, firing twice. "Head shot! He's down."

"Frag out!" a male voice yelled.

Talia tensed, preparing to catch and throw any object that flew through their doorway.

"That's our frag," said the female operative. "Time to grab one of those SMGs."

A thunderous crack shook the room, breaking plaster off the walls around the entrance and instantly filling the hallway with a cloud of dust. The operative changed positions, aiming her pistol toward the target suite at the end of the hallway.

The knife burned in Talia's hand. She could jam the small blade as far as possible into the woman's middle back and dash into the dust-choked hallway to grab one of her slain friends' weapons. She'd turn the suppressed HK UMP on the Hispanic operative and get the hell out of the hotel. The mission was screwed unless her sniper somehow got lucky. She paused as the debris settled.

"Are you gonna stab me in the back or help me kill Reznikov?" said the woman, without glancing in her direction.

"You're crazy," said Talia, sprinting through the doorway.

She emerged in time to see the Hispanic operative disappear into the Russian's off-duty guard suite. Several suppressed snaps from the room followed as she snagged both of the UMPs and dug through their blood-soaked clothing for spare magazines. A weak hand grabbed at her thigh, slipping back to the floor. Gilad was still alive—barely. He tried to speak, but a stream of blood poured out of his mouth. She glanced nervously over her shoulder at the woman that had shot Gilad, before leaning in close to him and whispering, "I'll get you out of here."

He shook his head and rasped, "Mission."

"Get out of the hallway," said the Hispanic CIA operative.

He crouched in the scarlet-splattered doorframe in front of her and leveled his weapon at the target suite. They had no intention of backing down—and neither did she.

"Time to put my best assets to work," she whispered back.

He smirked briefly before coughing uncontrollably. By the time she reached the perceived safety of the woman's suite, Gilad was silent.

Chapter 9

A sharp explosion rattled the walls, causing the Bratva security team to collectively flinch. Reznikov tried to pull away, but a firm hand kept him in place on the cool marble floor.

"You're going the wrong way," said Zuyev.

The gunfire in the hallway quieted after the explosion, a bad sign for the backup security team.

"Yergei," said Zuyev, "time to go."

Reznikov watched in horror as Yergei moved to the double doors, signaling silently for the team to form up around him.

"Going out there is suicide. You're supposed to keep me alive," pleaded Reznikov, straining against his grip. "I don't think Mr. Penkin would approve of this decision."

"If I'm wrong about this, it won't matter one way or the other," he said, yanking him closer.

He could smell Zuyev's lunch; garlic shrimp dominated the hot air spewing from his mouth less than an inch away. Reznikov felt nauseous.

"You stay right behind me. Understand? If you run, I'll shoot you in the spine and drag you out of here like a sack of dirty laundry. I'm only responsible for what's in here," said Zuyev, poking him in the forehead. "The rest of you is unimportant."

Holy shit! He was truly surrounded by psychopaths—not that this came to him as any revelation.

"Ready in three, two, one—" said Yergei, pulling on both door handles.

The men started firing before the doors fully opened, sending bullets through the thin wood into the hallway. Yergei's head snapped back before he could put his rifle into action, his body crumpling in place. The rest of the team scrambled past his lifeless, awkwardly sprawled corpse, steadily emptying their rifles' ninety-five-round-capacity drums in long bursts. Zuyev pulled him forward when the attackers' bullets stopped striking the wall behind the doorway.

Reznikov froze at the threshold, nearly pulling Zuyev off balance. Sharp cracks filled the air as the Bratva commander jerked him into the smoke-filled hallway.

"You're on your own now," said Zuyev, shouldering a drum-fed, short-barreled Saiga-12 semiautomatic shotgun.

Reznikov paused on the crimson-streaked marble, watching in disbelief as Zuyev fired the shotgun over and over again at the nearest open door. The shooters in the doorway disappeared in a shower of splinter fragments and plaster dust, emboldening the rest of the team to move forward in tight formation. Five of the original eight security guards remained, forming a compact shield of human flesh and bone. He followed Zuyev into the protective wedge, crouching as low as possible. The shotgun boomed, ejecting red-hot shells onto his head and shoulders.

A warm spray hit the right side of Reznikov's face, and the guard next to him dropped to both knees, clutching his neck. Bright red blood pumped through his fingers; a look of disbelief on his face. The gap was quickly filled by the next guard, who fired on full automatic into the room next to them. Zuyev's shotgun blasted over his head, pumping several shells into the same room as they passed. Deep inside the hotel suite, Reznikov caught a glimpse of long black hair whipping around a corner.

Chapter 10

Talia slid behind the kitchen island, immediately flipping onto her stomach. Jess, as the other operative called her, crouched behind a bullet-riddled wall across the opening exposed to the front door. The woman peeked around the corner, lifting the UMP and firing on full automatic toward the entrance.

"That's our target!" Jess yelled over the gunfire.

Without hesitating, Talia scooted forward and pressed the trigger, sending a fusillade of hastily aimed bullets toward the mass of khaki pants and short-sleeved shirts visible through the thinning dust. A man carrying an AK-74 stumbled backward, hit simultaneously by their barrage. He fell onto a man crouched behind him, shielding him from her next burst of fire. A shotgun barrel appeared on the right side of the doorway, filling the room with buckshot. She hated shotguns. Logically, a 5.45mm bullet to the face would be far more conclusive at this range, but the jackhammer boom of the semiautomatic shotgun and the resultant wall of lead forced her back.

Jess didn't flinch, even as some of the shot grazed her

exposed arm. She continued firing toward the door until the shotgun stopped.

"Let's go," she said, ejecting her spent magazine and picking up another from the floor.

The rifle gunfire intensified outside of the room, and Talia peeked around the base of the disintegrated kitchen island. The doorway appeared empty, but she wasn't inclined to charge into the open. Jess had no such reservations—or common sense. The CIA operative stood and moved forward, UMP jammed tight into her shoulder. As soon as she stepped into the hallway, the shotgun barrel materialized at the bottom of the door frame. She scrambled to her feet and leapt across the kill zone, tackling the impulsive operative to the ground—as dozens of lead balls buzzed inches behind her.

"Get off me!" said Jess, struggling underneath her.

"You'll get us both killed," said Talia, trying to hold her down.

She pushed Talia off, knocking her to the marble floor next to them. Before she could react, Jess was on her feet, slamming the bolt home on the UMP. The woman was single-minded and suicidal—a bad combination in the field.

"Hold it!" said Talia, springing into a crouch. "That shotgun will tear you to pieces."

The 12-gauge monster boomed outside of the room, sounding distant. Talia lined up behind and to the left of Jess, tapping her on the shoulder when she had a clear line of fire. They advanced together until they reached the doorway, Jess crouching low and Talia standing over her next to the splintered frame. Two dead Russians lay crumpled on the floor in front of the door. Three more cluttered the floor closer to the double entrance—not including the two she had killed before everything went to shit. The gunfire started to echo, like the shooters had moved into a tightly enclosed space.

"Stairwell," said Talia. "You ready?"

"Let's do this," said Jess, peeking around the corner with the UMP. "Clear."

They stepped out of the room, Jess aiming directly ahead of them at the stairwell entrance on the right side of the hallway; Talia covered the off-duty guard suite and the stairwell on the opposite side. A third guard sat propped against the right wall, his mangled head canted to the left at an extreme angle. A bright red stain covered the blue pastel wallpaper where his head should be. The gunfire died out completely, replaced with yelling from one of the stairwells. The Russians were on the move.

They stepped over Gilad's body, and Talia forced herself to stay focused on the scene ahead of them. Jess hesitated, stopping parallel to the guards' room.

"Any sign of my operative?" said Jess.

She peered into the smoky room, seeing nothing but shattered wood, bloodstained walls and collapsed bodies. Nothing moved.

"I can't tell," said Talia, her eye drawn to the stairwell door several feet away from the suite.

The metal fire door had been propped open at a ninety-degree angle to the wall; an empty rifle magazine jammed between the inside of the door and the frame.

Jess's shoulders slumped. She'd seen it too. The door was riddled with bullet holes.

"Munoz?" Jess yelled, keeping her weapon pointed at the opposite stairwell door.

"We need to move," said Talia. "They probably have a boat waiting for them."

Jess slid forward, stepping into the stairwell.

"Shit" she said, shaking her head. "All stations, Munoz is critically wounded in the poolside stairwell. Target has escaped down the beachside stairwell."

Talia moved forward far enough to see down the stairs. A thick pool of blood spread along the concrete landing, originating from the other CIA operative. Munoz must have been concealed behind the stairs, fighting desperately to keep the Russians from accessing the stairwell directly across the hall. Jess turned her head, keeping the UMP aimed forward.

"I have two of my people moving to intercept. Do you have more backup?" said Jess.

"Overwatch, this is assault. What is your status?" she said, pausing several seconds before tapping her earpiece. "Nothing. I think it's broken from our fight."

"Doesn't matter. We should have enough people to make this happen. I counted six down in the hallway and one just inside the target suite. Eight guards in a shift, plus Zuyev, Reznikov and the security chief. We're up against four at most," said Jess.

"Then what are we waiting for?" said Talia.

"Giving them some room. I don't want to be surprised on the stairs," said Jessica. "And I have someone moving into place that will be able to track them."

Talia nodded, wondering where Yoshi had gone. Without communications, Yoshi could complicate matters.

Chapter 11

The staccato sound of distant automatic gunfire resonated throughout the suite, drawing Daniel's attention toward the balcony. He mentally pictured the resort layout, concluding that Reznikov had three possible escape routes. Since they didn't have enough operatives to preemptively deny access to each option, he'd moved Melendez into a position to better determine the Russians' next move. Daniel would respond accordingly, working with a slim time margin to intercept the group. Jessica and her mystery "friend" would do the same. Everything hinged on Melendez's report.

"Rico, what are we seeing down there?" said Daniel.

"I'm not in position yet," said Melendez.

"Are you crawling there?" said Daniel.

"I'm moving as fast as I can without looking suspicious," said Melendez. "I'm the only one moving toward gunfire, and if you didn't notice, I'm wearing a Speedo."

"I've done my best not to notice," said Daniel, pausing. "We'll send someone back for Jeff."

"We need to focus on Reznikov," said Melendez.

"Right," said Daniel. "You good?"

"I learned from the best," said Melendez. "Hold on, I have something—targets entering the eastern gardens, heading north. Three armed men pulling a reluctant fourth along."

"Reznikov. I'll head toward the marina through the western gardens. We'll coordinate a two-pronged attack when I arrive," said Daniel, shouldering a tan backpack. "Jessica, what is your status?"

"Exiting the stairwell. We'll pick up the pace," she said.

"Watch your back," he said.

"I always do," said Jessica.

"Graves, how are we doing with the police response?" said Daniel, opening the suite door and quickly peeking outside.

All clear.

"Local authorities have been notified. They're coordinating a larger response with the city of Maldonado's metropolitan police force and the county's special response unit. Right now, Punta del Este police have units headed into blocking positions around the resort. Given the reports of automatic gunfire, I suspect they will hold those positions until reinforcements arrive. I give you ten to fifteen minutes before police start moving on the resort," said Graves.

"Is there any way to delay them?" said Daniel.

He pulled the private stairwell door with one hand, steadying the SOCOM 16 with the other. Clear.

"I could call and report a hostage situation, but that

would draw a lot of attention to the resort. Federal antiterrorism task force level attention."

"Do it. We'll need the buffer," said Daniel. "And start monitoring maritime frequencies. I don't want any surprises on the water."

"All clear so far," said Graves.

"One more thing," said Daniel. "Notify local paramedics that they have a gunshot victim in the poolside stairwell off the hallway leading to Reznikov's suite."

"Is that a good idea?" said Graves.

"Better he ends up in police custody than dead," said Daniel. "We can deal with police custody."

"Copy that," said Graves.

Daniel took the stairs two at a time. If he moved fast enough, he should be able to flank the Russians before they reached the hotel's private marina entrance. If not, they would take the fight to the floating docks—not an ideal situation for either group. He reached the ground floor and hit the glass door's crash bar with his left arm, holding the rifle in the other.

When Daniel pushed through the door, a figure stood to his right. Before he could react, his body stiffened, the crackling sound of electricity reaching his ears a fraction of a second too late for him to escape. A solid blow to his right forearm knocked the rifle loose; its synthetic polymer frame rattled behind him on the concrete floor. Unable to move, the figure slid behind him, pressing a blade under his chin.

Chapter 12

Enrique Melendez stumbled over an uneven stone in the walking path, pitching forward before quickly regaining his balance.

"Son of mother," he mumbled, hoping the sudden movement didn't attract the Russians' attention.

Not that they would have given him a second glance. He was dressed in a skimpy turquoise Speedo-type suit. A "banana hammock" they had called it at West Point, where far less stylish versions had been standard issue for the freshman class. When he'd enthusiastically placed his "hammock" in the trash at the end of plebe year, he never imagined he'd wear one again under any circumstances. Wrong again.

At least he wasn't wearing one of those thongy things making the scene. Jessica had suggested he adopt the newest Mediterranean beach craze, no doubt to further humiliate him, but Jeff intervened. The Speedo was bad enough, he had told her, sharing a smirk with her. They always messed with him, especially Jeff.

He refused to believe the guy was gone. No time to

process that now. He couldn't afford to let the rage building inside to cloud his judgment. His situation was precarious, requiring concentration to stay alive. Dressed in nothing but a Speedo and leather sandals, he wasn't in a position to make a useful difference with the suppressed pistol tucked into his straw beach bag. Not yet. For now, he was the eyes and ears of the team. The rage could come later.

He kept them at a distance, doing his best to put as much lush foliage between himself and the heavily armed men as possible. Even if he caught their attention, he couldn't imagine they would perceive him as much of a threat. Not dressed like this. Then again, Solntsevskaya Bratva thugs didn't need a rational reason to kill someone, especially under the circumstances. His best bet was to stay out of sight.

Out of the corner of his eye, he spotted Jessica and a woman dressed in a hotel uniform sprinting down one of the easternmost paths—apparently obscured from the Russians. He checked on the Russians again, seeing them turn right toward the central path leading to the marina. Running the map of the resort's grounds through his head, he determined that they would pass through the marina entrance before Jessica could intercept. Unless Daniel was close to setting up an ambush position from the western side of the gardens, Melendez was about to make program history—in a Speedo.

"Jess, you're gaining ground, but it won't be enough to intercept," said Melendez. "Daniel, are you in position?"

Jessica waited a few seconds before responding. "Something's wrong. Daniel's comms worked fine a minute ago."

"We don't have time to figure that out," said Melendez. "I have to slow down the Russians."

"I don't think that's a smart idea," said Jessica. "You're outgunned and underdressed."

"Funny," said Melendez. "I'm buying you and your new friend some time. I suggest you take a more direct approach."

"Rico, just give us a second—"

Graves spoke over her radio transmission.

"All stations, I have two go-fast boats approaching the marina. Each boat is loaded with armed men. Whatever you're planning to do, you better do it now. They can pull those right up to the docks."

"Engaging," said Melendez. "Get your asses in position."

He ignored Jessica's whispered curses as he pulled two spare 9mm magazines from the straw bag and tucked them into the left side of his barely stretchable swimsuit. With the extra magazines in place, he gripped the HK USP and let the bag fall to the ground behind him. Dashing forward, he settled in behind a thick palm trunk and centered the pistol sights on the partially obscured group more than fifty yards away.

A red blotch appeared in the cluster of shirts, followed by yelling and gunfire. Melendez pressed against the palm, exposing enough of his face to gauge the Russians' response. Given the fact that the palm wasn't taking repeated hits, he guessed that they didn't know his location.

The men crouched low, firing on full automatic. Screams erupted from the hotel: resort guests responding to the renewed shooting spree. The flowers and bushes around them danced and snapped for a few moments until a harsh order instantly silenced the guns. They were disciplined. Many of them were former Russian Special Forces, making them all the more dangerous.

When the group started moving again, Melendez crouched and sprinted to a tree trunk down the path, staying below the foliage line. Hitting the rough palm bark with his left shoulder, he peeked around the corner with the pistol and squeezed off three bullets in their direction. The tree thudded with return fire, the Russians now wise to his position. He squatted lower, not wanting to test the palm's resistance to a heavy volume of high-velocity bullets. He'd seen similar calibers penetrate harder woods after repeat hits.

The sound of the gunfire shifted, initially confusing him. For a moment, he thought a second group of Russians had joined the fight. A quick glance around the opposite side of the tree revealed that some of the Bratva guards were firing in a different direction.

"They stopped our approach," said Jessica.

"I see that," said Melendez, firing the rest of his magazine. "I don't have a good view of their group. What are they doing?"

Suppressed gunshots competed with the automatic fusillade.

"They're shooting at us," she said. "From covered positions. I don't think this is going to work."

"Hold on," he said, hoping they were distracted enough by Jessica's fire.

Melendez slid around the tree, heading down the path with a freshly reloaded pistol. Bullets whipped through the leaves lining the walkway in front of him, rapidly moving toward him. He fired his pistol and dove for the stone surface, scraping the skin off his knees and elbows. Projectiles fanned the bushes next to him, miraculously staying a few inches above his back.

"This is going to hurt," he muttered, low-crawling toward the nearest tree.

"They're moving!" said Jessica.

A long burst of gunfire penetrated the bushes around him.

"Doesn't sound like it," said Melendez. "I'm completely pinned down."

"I think they left two behind to slow us down," said Jessica. "Graves, what are you seeing?"

"One boat speeding toward the inner marina. Six armed men on board," said Graves. "The other boat is holding outside the entrance."

"We're going to push through, Rico," said Jessica. "Reload and get ready to empty your pistol."

"Where the hell is Daniel?" said Melendez, thinking out loud.

"No time to think about that," said Jessica. "We move in three. Two."

Melendez reloaded the pistol and fired the entire

magazine at a rapid, sustained pace—never hearing the end of the countdown. The return fire was sporadic, indicating that they had caused some damage.

"One down. One wounded," said Jessica. "We're coming at him from two directions."

Melendez reloaded his pistol with the last magazine in his Speedo, while the furious gun battle continued. Intermittent torrents of AK-74 gunfire mixed with quieter suppressed cracks, leading him to believe that the guard's full attention was devoted to the two women trying to kill him. He sprinted forward during the guard's next extended burst, staying low to avoid detection. The next tree stood adjacent to the central garden valley, giving him an unobstructed view across the entire north-south axis of the resort.

He glanced behind at the hotel, catching a glimpse of smoke drifting from the upper level of the eastern wing. A few people dressed in bathing suits or hotel uniforms dashed back and forth across the pool deck, dodging pool chairs and tables. With no threat inbound from the hotel, he turned his focus to the marina entrance.

Roughly seventy yards away, the gardens opened to the glistening, dark blue water of the bay superimposed with a sprawling dock system. Two men, one with a bloodied shirt, stumbled onto the wide stone walkway, pausing momentarily. The bloodied man swept a shortened AK-74 back and forth, checking for pursuers, before shoving the other man toward the marina. Melendez waited until both of their backs had turned before bracing the pistol against the tree and aligning the pistol's sights center of mass on the unarmed Russian. *This will be one hell of a shot*, he thought, pressing the trigger.

Both men spun immediately, the bloodied man spraying bullets down the central path. Melendez had missed—not a surprise given the range. Bullets thunked into the tree from Jessica's direction, causing him to drop to the stone and flatten his body. The palm trunk wasn't thick enough to block bullets from two directions. Moments later, the gardens fell silent.

"Target down. Thanks for the distraction," said Jessica. "We're moving to your location. Where's Reznikov?"

"Marina entrance. Be careful approaching the central path. I'll try to hold them in place."

Melendez peeked around the tree, drawing aimed fire from the shooter near the marina entrance. The stones next to his face chipped, spraying his face and right shoulder with sharp fragments. He squinted and fired toward the source of gunfire, hoping to keep the shooter in place until Jessica arrived. A few seconds later, Graves brought them some bad news.

"Two men just barreled through the marina gate. They'll be gone in less than thirty seconds," said Graves.

Jessica burst onto the central path, firing her UMP on fully automatic toward the gate. Her newly found partner, an exotic, dark-haired femme fatale, stopped in the middle of the path, firing on semiautomatic. In the distance, their bullets clanged against metal and shattered glass in the marina guard shack.

"We won't make it," said Jessica.

"This is your backup?" said the other woman.

Jessica turned to look at him. "Good god. Talia, meet Rico."

"I told you the Speedo was a stupid idea," he said.

"Better than the man thong," she said, tossing a loaded AKS-74U rifle at him.

He snatched it out of the air, still grumbling as they took off for the marina.

Chapter 13

Timothy Graves hesitated. He knew it was a seriously flawed idea, but what choice did he have? He tore his headset off and stood up, throwing them on the steel desk in front of his chair.

"I'm going out there," he said.

"It's like ninety-five degrees outside," said Anish Gupta, closely studying the three screens arrayed in front of him.

Graves unzipped the long black nylon duffel bag sitting on the couch behind the communications suite and dug through the bag. Gupta's head swiveled at the sound of metal scraping against polymer, his eyes going wide.

"That's not what we get paid to do," he said.

"We're part of the team," said Graves, removing a short-barreled M4 rifle equipped with an EOTech holographic sight.

"That is a really bad idea," said Gupta, trying to divide his attention between Graves and the screens. "And you can barely fire one of those."

"I'm better with this than you think," said Graves, inserting a magazine and charging the weapon.

Through the tinted windows lining the yacht's communications suite, he saw the fast boat plying through the crowded water of the inner marina. He needed to do something within the next several seconds. With a quick flick of his thumb, he changed the selector switch from safe to semiautomatic.

"Dude, you're black hat, not black ops," said Gupta.

"I just need to slow them down," said Graves, slipping a few spare magazines into his cargo pockets.

"That's the definition of a speed bump," said Gupta, pushing his glasses up his nose.

Graves rushed toward the open hatch leading to the bridge, his eyes tracking the boat through the long window.

"You're serious," stated Gupta, now half standing and half sitting.

"You're the team's eyes and ears now," said Graves, stepping through the hatch.

"Shit!" said Gupta, immediately passing Graves's intentions to the team.

He opened the bridge wing door and stepped into the stifling heat, perspiration immediately forming on his face. The last thing he heard before the door closed was Gupta yelling something about "Jessica denied your request."

Standing on the starboard side of the upper deck, he was shaded from the sun by the flying bridge level above him. He kept the rifle low and jogged aft, watching the boat approach the two men. They scrambled down the first branching pier on the left side of the hotel marina, searching for an empty slip long enough to accommodate the craft. Not finding one close enough, they started down one of the slip dividers, headed for the end, where the boat could come alongside. The man with the rifle appeared wounded, the entire left side of his white, short-sleeved shirt stained dark red. The boat driver adjusted to the Russian's strategy, speeding toward the end of the divider.

Jessica's group hadn't reached the marina gate when the bow of the sleek cigarette boat passed the end of the dock. Graves immediately stopped, steadying his rifle on the varnished wood handrail and searching through the holographic sight for the boat. The boat came into view through the unmagnified EOTech, but he didn't see the green sight reticle—because he hadn't powered the device.

"Shit," he muttered, briefly wondering if Gupta had been right.

The bloodied Russian dropped his rifle on the pier, grabbing the other man as the boat eased alongside. Graves put the boat in the middle of the rectangular picture and pressed the trigger. The rifle bucked into his shoulder, a sensation he never seemed to anticipate correctly. By the time he reacquired the boat, bullets started to puncture the thin metal superstructure next to him with a hollow popping sound. He pressed the trigger repeatedly as glass shattered behind him and the wooden railing splintered.

A sharp pain fired up his right arm, followed by an odd sensation in his hips. His left hand still held the rifle as he helplessly stumbled backward into the superstructure. Graves slid down the side, his legs and feet extending neatly in front of him as his bottom came to rest against the scorching teak deck. He glanced at his right arm long enough to know that it had been mangled by a bullet that passed through his elbow. Any attempt to do more with the arm than shrug his shoulder was rejected. Same with his legs. They moved, which was a good thing, but didn't obey his commands. He was essentially stuck sitting against the superstructure with bullets hitting all around him.

Over his shoulder, he saw that his efforts had done little to stop the boarding process. The two Russians on the pier had temporarily taken cover behind one of the waist-high pilings, but were trying to board the boat again. Bullets pinged off the handrail supports, sparking as they ricocheted into the teak deck. With supersonic cracks passing inches from his face, he used the rifle to push himself onto his right side. He fell over, landing flat on his stomach, which luckily put him in the position he wanted. If he'd toppled onto his back, he would have been stuck like a turtle.

Graves inched forward far enough to slide the rifle over the metal toe rail and brace the weapon against one of the vertical stanchions. He eased his left hand over the pistol grip and leaned his head behind the EOTech sight. The rifle trembled from the excruciating pain in his arm, making it difficult to find his target. When he finally regained the previous sight picture, Reznikov's hand extended across the two-foot gap between the pier and the boat, stretching to reach one of the hands eager to pull him on board.

He pressed the trigger in panic, seeing the bullet strike the glass in front of the driver. The boat lurched forward at full throttle, striking the main pier moments later with a devastating crunch. Graves lowered his head to the blood-slicked deck, listening to the gunfire intensify on the dock. He'd given the team a chance.

Chapter 14

The pier buckled under her feet from the force of an unseen impact, knocking Jessica off balance. Talia caught her by the arm, steadying her before continuing down the pier.

"Slow down," said Jessica, turning to give a hand signal to Melendez.

The group spread out, moving from piling to piling toward the source of panicked shouting down the pier. She assumed that Graves had somehow wrecked the boat. The cigarette boat's powerful engines roared just before the pier shook, indicating a crash. If the boat was disabled, they had a good chance of ending this in the marina.

The pier system didn't leave many options for escape without a working boat, unless you were willing to get wet. She somehow doubted Zuyev would take that chance with Reznikov. Neither struck her as proficient swimmers. She carefully advanced down the pier, searching for the Russians with no success. The dock was crowded with luxury sailboats and cabin cruisers, completely blocking her view of the access piers. The best she could hope for was a quick spotting between boats.

She glanced at the massive yacht ahead and to the right, searching for signs of Graves. The second deck aft had taken the brunt of the Bratva's gunfire. Half of the long, tinted windows lining the superstructure were shattered, dozens of bullet holes evident underneath the jagged openings. A blood splatter was visible against the white metal superstructure, just above a protruding rifle barrel. Graves was down.

"Gupta, I need you—"

Gunfire interrupted her sentence, bullets clacking into the wood piling in front of her. Talia and Melendez immediately returned fire, their bullets tearing into the fiberglass hull of a squat motorboat four piers down. Jessica leaned around the piling, searching for a target. The Russians popped up and fired at staggered intervals, making it nearly impossible to return a properly aimed burst. She counted at least three different shooters, leading her to believe the Russians had managed to offload reinforcements before the crash.

"We're not making any progress!" said Talia.

Jessica pressed the UMP against the right side of the piling and waited. A Russian peeked around the corner of the motorboat, firing a quick burst at her, but she didn't flinch—or adjust her sight picture to fire at him. By the time she moved her weapon, he would be gone. She waited. Moments later, a shooter rose above the stern, appearing off-center from the red dot in her reflex sight. She nudged the weapon right and fired a single shot, catching the man on his way down. A splash of red exploded behind his head before he vanished behind the boat.

"How's that?" replied Jessica, the piling in front of her absorbing another hail of bullets.

"Not bad, but we need to move forward before the next boat arrives!" yelled Talia over the booming of Melendez's rifle.

She was right. All the Russians had to do was keep them busy long enough to put Reznikov on the second boat. Time wasn't on their side.

"Melendez, I need some tight firing while we move up!" said Jessica.

"I have about forty rounds left in this drum, so you better make it happen soon," he said, firing a short burst. "Thirty-seven."

"Moving," said Jessica, sliding around the piling.

Melendez and Talia fired simultaneously, suppressing the Russians long enough for her to reach a double piling at the head of the next pier branch. She glanced down the long row of boats to her left, making sure their flank was clear. Graves didn't think the cigarette boat stopped at one of the closer piers, but she couldn't trust her life to his assessment, even though he had demonstrated an unusual aptitude for tactical decision making a few minutes ago.

"Clear!" she said, squeezing off three successive bursts of .45-caliber bullets at the Russians.

Talia slammed into the wooden posts on the opposite side of the main pier, drawing an angry beehive of rifle fire.

"Three more piers to go!" said Jessica.

"They won't make it easy on us," replied Talia. "One more pier, and they'll adjust."

Jessica fired a long burst and dropped to one knee, reloading the UMP.

"Then we'll adjust with them," she said. "Rico, can you swim with a rifle?"

"Not very fast," he said. "I didn't grow up with a pool."

"Like all of the white Serbian princesses you know?" said Jessica, slapping the weapon's bolt home.

"White privilege is a bitch," said Melendez, firing two rapid shots down the pier.

A thickly muscled Bratva soldier stumbled onto the central pier, holding his neck. Jessica and Talia reacted immediately, sprinting forward while firing. The man shook from multiple .45-caliber impacts, dropping to his knees. Melendez fired a single shot that struck his forehead, snapping his head back. The body remained upright for a few seconds before toppling sideways with a heavy thud. A rifle poked over the top of the motorboat's stern, wildly spraying the pier.

"Rico, keep up the pressure on the last shooter," she said, walking briskly forward with her weapon leveled at the corner of the boat.

With all three of them firing every time the remaining Russian tried to fire, they managed to cross two more piers before stopping to strategize how to approach the docked motorboat. They had reached the point where moving any closer exposed them to fire from the well-

covered position behind the boat. The Russian could fire
on them without risking a bullet to the head from
Melendez. Talia nodded once, giving her a "what's next?"
look.

She peeked around the thick wooden post, expecting
to see the business end of a rifle. Instead, the marina
quieted. She listened intently over the ringing in her ears
from the gunfire, hearing a faint thumping sound.

"They're on the move," she said, stepping into the
open. "Cover me."

Jessica reached the top of the shooter's pier
unopposed, swinging the barrel of the UMP around the
stern of the motorboat. Several boats away, the same two
men she'd seen leave the hotel's central garden scrambled
toward a waiting boat at the far end of the pier. The man
with the bloodstained shirt turned and fired his rifle on
full automatic with one hand, his other holding a cell
phone. She quickly stepped back, the bullets rattling off
the pier and boats docked between them. Talia sprinted
across the pier, barely avoiding a second burst of gunfire.

"Do you hear that?" yelled Talia.

"Get ready to fire. They're thirty meters out!" said
Jessica, ignoring Talia's question.

She moved a few feet beyond the stern of the boat and
crouched, rapidly acquiring the back of Reznikov's yellow
shirt. Before she pressed the trigger, the faint thumping
she had mistaken for footsteps turned to thunder, and the
Russians flattened themselves on the pier. A silver-gray
helicopter roared past the trees lining the cove beyond
the awaiting cigarette boat. She fired once at her quarry

before instinctively turning the UMP skyward.

The helicopter yawed left and appeared to skid in the air toward her, exposing the open starboard-side passenger compartment. Two men sat on the edge of the compartment floor, with their feet on the skids—firing light machine guns. Jessica reacted instantly, dropping into the water between the pier and the bullet-riddled motorboat.

Jessica pressed her arms against the sides of her body and bore through the water like a torpedo, sinking as far below the surface as possible. Her world had been instantly quieted under water, intensifying the shrill ringing in her ears. The salt water burned her eyes, but she forced them open to search for the nearest submerged pier footing. Finding one nearby, she dropped the submachine gun and wrapped her arms around the sharp, barnacle-encrusted post.

Bullets hit the pier above her, sounding like a muted woodpecker underwater, the staccato impacts vibrating through the submerged piling she embraced. She held tight as dozens of bullets swished through the water next to the pier, travelling erratically until they lost all velocity and drifted to the bottom of the marina.

Her lungs burned from the excess carbon dioxide buildup, but she stayed under until the bullets stopped, and the sound of a powerful engine dominated her ears. She slowly rose along the post as the underwater vibration weakened. The cigarette boat was headed out. Jessica delayed breaching the surface until the spasms in her trachea and ribs threatened a forced inhalation of water. Her mouth found air first, greedily sucking in a short breath. The rest of her head followed as she normalized her breathing and scanned the marina.

"What are you, a free diver in your spare time?" said Talia, holding on to a metal ladder leading up to a wooden trapdoor. "I almost swam down to get you. The helicopter's gone. So is the boat."

"Shit," hissed Jessica, her mind swimming with conflicting thoughts.

Daniel was nowhere to be found. Munoz was critically wounded. Graves was likely dead on a bullet-riddled yacht that was supposed to remain a secret. And she didn't trust this woman not to cut her throat in the water.

"We need to get out of here," said Talia, climbing the ladder.

"You think?" said Jessica, scissor kicking toward her. "First priority is finding my other operative. Second is getting the yacht out of here."

"First priority is going after Reznikov," said Talia.

"The op is done," said Jessica, grasping the slick ladder.

"I didn't lose half of my team just to give up. My mission remains intact," said Talia, pushing on the trapdoor with her right hand.

"Good luck with that," said Jessica. "I'm cutting my losses here."

The trapdoor opened suddenly, causing Talia to slip a few rungs on the ladder.

"Don't shoot," said Melendez, slowly easing his face into view. "We need to get out of here muy pronto, ladies. Gupta deep-sixed all of the laptops. He's trying to figure out how to launch the yacht's tender."

"I need to find Daniel," said Jessica.

"Daniel can take care of himself," said Melendez. "Graves is critically injured. We need to get him to a private medical facility. We're thirty-five minutes by boat to one of our planned fall-back points. La Paloma Marina. We can transfer Graves to a car there and drive him fifteen minutes inland to a private doctor in Rocha."

"You need to use that boat to pursue Reznikov," said Talia, climbing onto the pier.

"And get lit up by their helicopter?" said Jessica, emerging through the trapdoor. "What part of mission scratched don't you understand?"

"That's it, then?" said Talia.

"That's it," said Jessica, turning her back.

"The fearless CIA just folds on a mission?" challenged Talia.

"We're not really CIA or any agency for that matter," said Jessica.

"Then I guess killing *Daniel* won't be a problem between our countries," said Talia.

Jessica stiffened. Something was off. Her suspicion was immediately confirmed when Talia smirked, tapping her ear.

"My earpiece is fine," she said, walking toward her. "Daniel was taken by my people when he exited the western wing of the hotel—carrying a SOCOM 16 rifle."

"You bitch!" snapped Jessica, rushing toward her.

"No time for that," said Talia, holding up a hand. "Here's the deal. You and Speedo agree to help me take down Reznikov and Zuyev, and your operative leaves the hotel in an ambulance driven by my people. If not, he leaves in a body bag with the medical examiner."

Jessica bristled at the threat. "I'll dedicate the rest of my life to killing you."

"Join the club," said Talia, glancing back at the hotel. "Time's ticking."

"You get my other operative out in the same ambulance," said Jessica. "And we have a deal."

"If it's not too late," said Talia, waiting a few seconds. "I've just been told they can get him out."

"Then we have a deal," said Jessica. "But what makes you think we can help you find the Russians?"

"I know an off-the-books CIA op when I see one. You may not get a monthly paycheck from Langley, but I'm guessing you know people that can make shit happen," said Talia. "The Russians will go to ground at a safe house in Montevideo or Buenos Aires. We need to figure out where they're headed."

"And your agency doesn't have resources?" said Jessica.

"I can assemble a strike team within a few hours, but we lack wide-scale intelligence regarding worldwide Solntsevskaya Bratva activities. Any help would be appreciated."

Jessica glanced at Melendez, who nodded his approval.

"I'll get the ball rolling," said Jessica.

PART TWO

BLACKOUT

Chapter 15

Karl Berg's cell phone buzzed, displaying an anxiously awaited number. He'd just received a call from Audra Bauer requesting an immediate status update on the Uruguay operation. Sanderson had been stingy with the details surrounding the take down, which didn't sit well with him or Audra. Reznikov's continued ability to draw oxygen represented a serious black eye for the agency, not to mention a clear and present danger to the world. The investigation into his escape from custody pointed directly at the Solntsevskaya Bratva. A painful revelation given the Bratva's involvement in Berg's plan to destroy Vektor Institute.

He should have known better than to trust an organization built around a "thieves' code." Technically, the Bratva had honored their word, enabling Sanderson's team of operatives to wipe out the Russian Federation's secret and highly illegal bioweapons program. They had jacked up the price at the last minute like any thief would, but he'd been ready for that—had built it into the budget. What he hadn't anticipated was a complete end run by the Bratva to steal the grand prize right under his nose. Pure genius on every level, which led back to Reznikov.

Bratva leadership was crafty—not crazy. Breaking into a heavily defended CIA compound to retrieve a man at the top of every nation's watch list was the definition of crazy. Something tipped the scales, and he was willing to bet Reznikov had planted that seed long before his capture. What else was growing out there? Nothing good, he thought, swiping the phone from his cluttered desk. He hoped this call represented the end of a very ugly chapter in his CIA career.

"Tell me he's dead," said Berg, holding his breath.

"We ran into an unexpected complication," said a vaguely familiar female voice.

"Nicole?" he said.

"I prefer Jessica," she said.

"Uh-huh. How complicated—Jessica?" said Berg, not sure why he wasn't communicating directly with Sanderson.

"On a scale of one to ten, I'd give this a ten," said Jessica.

"Where's the general?" said Berg, starting to feel flush.

Something was way off here.

"Sanderson told me to deal with you directly on this," she said. "Reznikov escaped."

"Fuck," whispered Berg. "That's more than a complication. How the hell did this happen? The intelligence was up to date and verified by a highly trusted source."

"We didn't have a problem with the target intel. We had a problem with the Mossad team sent to kill Zuyev," she said. "It got a little crowded at the resort."

What the hell was she talking about? Mossad? They weren't even looking for Reznikov. Shit. Zuyev had been photographed with the Iranians recently. What were the chances of a simultaneous operation? Double Shit. Their intelligence source had double-dipped. Both agencies had been tipped off simultaneously.

"Jessica, what exactly happened at the resort?"

"The Mossad team hit Reznikov's suite at the same time," said Jessica.

"As in the same exact time?" said Berg.

"As in Jeff and Graves are seriously wounded. We're hiding out in some country shithole in Uruguay. Both Russian targets escaped. And the Mossad has Daniel," she recited.

"How do you know the other team is Mossad?" he said.

"I'm standing next to one of their operatives right now. Calls herself Talia," she replied.

A female voice protested in the background of Jessica's phone call.

"You took one of their operatives hostage?" said Berg.

"Not exactly," she said.

"Not exactly?" said Berg.

"It's complicated," said Jessica.

"I keep hearing that," said Berg. "I'll make a few calls and get Daniel released. I suggest you send the Mossad agent on her way—unharmed. We don't need any bad blood with the Israelis."

"It's more complicated than that," said Jessica.

"You're starting to sound like a broken record," said Berg.

"I need a big favor. No questions asked," said Jessica.

Berg hesitated. The answer should have come instantly, but part of him still couldn't forgive her for putting him through hell for all of those years. Countless days and nights spent second-guessing his decision to fast-track her deployment as a deep-cover agent in the Balkans. Years of blaming himself for the brutal murder of Nicole Erak, an idealistic young woman unable to escape the demons of her troubled upbringing—no matter how hard she tried. Years believing a lie.

"I should hang up and cut my losses with a completely botched mission," said Berg.

"But you won't," she said.

Berg detected a hint of doubt in her voice.

"No. I won't," he said. "What do you need?"

"My new Mossad friend strongly suspects that the Russians will hide Reznikov in Buenos Aires or Montevideo until they can guarantee his safe passage out of the area. The Israelis can put together a strike team, if we can find Reznikov," said Jessica.

"I don't have a worldwide directory to Solntsevskaya safe houses, Jessica," said Berg.

"What about the FBI?" she said.

"They weren't much help investigating Reznikov's escape—especially in South America," said Berg.

"I need you to dig deep on this one, Karl," said Jessica. "As deep as Stockholm."

"What do you mean?" said Berg, understanding perfectly.

"That intel didn't come from the CIA," she said.

That was all he needed to hear. All he wanted to hear. Kaparov was one of his most closely guarded secrets. Somehow she knew.

"That's a serious long shot," said Berg.

"I need you to take it," said Jessica. "Please."

"Don't ever hint about Stockholm again," he said.

"I don't know what you're talking about," she said.

"Exactly," he said, disconnecting the call.

He glanced at the time on his phone. 1:48 PM. 8:48 in Moscow. Not too late to place a call to an old enemy—turned friend.

Chapter 16

Thick tendrils of bluish-gray smoke curled upward from the ashtray on his nightstand, dispersing above the yellow, nicotine-stained lampshade. Kaparov took a long belt of vodka straight from a bottle and rested the half-empty glass flagon next to him on the mattress—his fingers clutched its neck.

He sweated profusely. Not because of a record Moscow heat wave or the barely functional window air conditioner precariously installed in his bedroom window. He perspired lying in bed because he was "in bad health," as his doctors liked to put it. Diabetes, thyroid issues and obesity all contributed to his perpetual state of sweating—along with a host of other problems he could care less about.

He reached over to retrieve the cigarette, pausing to stare at the television screen. Some inane Russian reality show had come on nearly an hour ago, but he didn't feel like getting up to change the channel. The remote was even further away, deposited on his dresser during his last trip to the bathroom. He was starting to see double, so it really didn't matter what was on the television. His hand found the cigarette and started to drift to his mouth; in a ritual he repeated several hundred times a day. An annoying ringtone jarred him out of his trance.

Kaparov took an angry pull on the cigarette, blowing the smoke through his nostrils as he stormed out of the bedroom. They had low-level agents on duty for this kind of shit. He should be the last person called, not the first—regardless of the crisis. Every night was the same now. The calls started after eight, invariably pulling him out of bed to learn that unreliable contact in east-fuckistan thinks he overheard a hashish-wasted, wannabe militia shitstain talking about a Russian.

He was going out of his mind with this nonsense! Despite SVR claims that Reznikov was dead, a fact he knew to be untrue, his life consisted of one Reznikov false alarm after another—compliments of the SVR! He grabbed the phone from his kitchen counter, not bothering to check the caller ID.

"Kaparov. Print a copy of the report and place it on my desk. This is why I drink!" he yelled into the phone, disconnecting the call and turning away from the counter.

The phone rang again before he reached the bedroom door.

"I'm going to kill someone," he said, flipping open the phone and seeing the caller ID.

He recognized the Moscow prefix, but the number was not one of the FSB duty desk extensions.

"Kaparov," he said, as calmly as he could muster.

"Alexei, I hope I didn't wake you," said a voice he had hoped to never hear again.

Actually, that wasn't true. Deep down inside, he would like nothing more than to meet Karl Berg again—in person, preferably at a posh bar where the American's credit card provided endless liquor to fuel their Cold War stories. Unfortunately, Berg's phone calls had come to represent one thing. Bad news. Each call usually worse than the last.

"No. You caught me at the perfect time. I was about to blow my brains out with my service pistol. I'm sure whatever you are about to propose equates to the same thing," he said.

"I see your sense of humor remains intact," said Berg.

"Miraculously, my head remains intact, no thanks to you," said Kaparov. "To what do I owe the pleasure of your voice? I assume this isn't a social call. I'm still waiting on that drink you promised."

"One of these days, my friend, and I mean that," said Berg.

"Sounds like you're buttering me up," said Kaparov, extinguishing the cigarette in his bedside ashtray and retrieving the bottle he had propped against the pillow. "Time for another drink."

"I can barely understand you as it is," said Berg.

"I'm only on my second bottle," said Kaparov.

"At that rate, you won't remember this conversation in the morning," said Berg.

"Precisely," said Kaparov, taking a long pull on the bottle. "What can I do for you?"

"Is this line secure?" said Berg.

"As secure as one can expect in Moscow," said Kaparov, laughing at his own joke. "It's secure. I would know."

"We almost caught him," said Berg.

Kaparov dropped the bottle on the bed, quickly grabbing it to prevent any of the precious liquid from spilling.

"Almost?" he said.

"We caught his Bratva benefactors off guard, but something very unexpected ruined the operation," said Berg.

"This couldn't wait until morning? I won't be able to sleep now. What the hell happened?" said Kaparov, placing the bottle next to the smoldering ashtray.

"It was a mess, that's all I know," said Berg. "But we still have a chance to find him."

"Go on," said Kaparov.

"It's going to take some digging—on your part," said Berg. "We suspect he's holed up with the Solntsevskaya Bratva somewhere near Buenos Aires. Possibly Montevideo."

"Fortunately for you, I know exactly where to dig," said Kaparov, pausing. "First thing in the morning."

Chapter 17

Alexei Kaparov paid for a venti cappuccino and a tall dark roast coffee, smiling politely as he handed over a princely sum to the sickly looking youngster working the register at the American-based coffee house chain—one of three located within a five-minute walk of Lubyanka Square. *And Putin tells us we won the Cold War.* He eyeballed the clear plastic tip container with contempt, grumbling as he shuffled to the end of the counter to wait with the rest of the government crowd. Five minutes later, he was on the street, headed south on Bulshaya Lubyanka Boulevard.

Shades of gray and brown dominated the suits filing by, perfectly matching the thoroughly uninspired, squat buildings surrounding him. Oddly enough, the historic Lubyanka was the most colorful building on the square, with its yellow brick façade. He never understood how it survived Stalin's era without a thorough facelift. Neo-Baroque architecture, though modestly displayed in the construction of the Lubyanka building, represented grandeur and opulence, along with implicit religious undertones. Everything the Bolsheviks claimed to despise, supposedly. Maybe the party was too stupid to realize the significance of the architecture by that point. The purges had likely eliminated anyone that could identify it. The purges gave Russians half a century of ten-story, rectangular gray concrete abominations. No wonder we drink so much.

Holding the two coffees, he turned right on Pushechnaya Boulevard and strolled through an unattended black, wrought-iron gate. A small, featureless courtyard led to one of FSB Headquarters' unmarked entrances, reserved for deputy director level and above. In true Russian bureaucratic style, the heavily guarded access points saw little traffic. Most of the FSB senior leadership drove their own cars or were assigned drivers, entering the massive building through the parking garage.

He negotiated the different security stations with ease, being one of the entrance's repeat customers throughout the day. He strolled Lubyanka Square several times a day when he didn't feel like smoking in the confines of his office. Upon entering the main building, he joined the procession of grim-faced agents and staff cramming themselves onto elevators to hasten the start of their ten-hour day. He purposely waited for an elevator car that didn't hold anyone from his department, refusing politely and blaming the coffees when a space was offered. His first stop of the day would not be his own office within the Bioweapons/Chemical Threat Assessment Division.

Arriving on the fourth floor, he wove through a maze of hallways and cubicle farms, enduring the unsure glances and uncomfortable stares of agents unfamiliar with his face, but very familiar with the deputy director markings on his security badge. He nodded and returned greetings from the few agents that had enough guts to address him. Everything and nothing had changed from the old days. During the iron reign of the KGB, subordinates stumbled over each other to be the first to address a senior-ranking agent—out of fear. Now they shrank into corners or pretended you were invisible, for the same reason. He wasn't sure which system was worse.

He found the office he sought on the outer edge of a small cluster of open workstations, half occupied with agents and support staff. The rest would arrive in the next fifteen minutes, ready to brief the division's deputy director. He glanced at the black placard next to the door: Assistant Deputy Director Yuri Prerovsky, Organized Crime Division. He knocked on the door, which was cracked open a few inches.

"Come in," said his former assistant.

Kaparov nudged the door with one of the coffees, steeling himself for a less than enthusiastic reunion. The two of them hadn't exchanged more than a few required pleasantries during chance elevator encounters since Yuri's reassignment—on the heels of his girlfriend's "disappearance." Lucya Pavrikova's involuntary defection to the United States had been a messy affair that nearly consumed both Prerovsky and Kaparov.

They'd done the right thing for Lucya, the Russian Federation and themselves, but the events surrounding her abduction created a strain in their working relationship. Kaparov pulled a few strings to get

Prerovsky a promotion outside of the department. A move he felt necessary for Prerovsky's continued growth within the FSB. And frankly, he couldn't bear to look at the man's long, guilty face in the office any longer. They both needed to move on from the whole Reznikov incident, which is why he expected this to be a tough conversation.

"Alexei!" said Prerovsky, quickly moving around an uncluttered, perfectly organized desk to greet him. "This is a pleasant surprise."

The brown-haired, meticulously dressed agent took the coffees from his hand and placed them on the desk before embracing him in a warm, Russian hug.

"Seriously, it's good to see you," said Prerovsky, stepping back and pulling a chair closer. "Please, take a seat. Do I smell a cappuccino?"

Kaparov dropped into the institutionally uncomfortable plastic chair and pushed the beverage across the desk. He closed the door with one hand, taking the small coffee with the other.

"I've never been a fan of this new open-door policy," said Kaparov.

"I should have known," said Prerovsky, eyeing the cappuccino suspiciously. "You're too cheap to buy coffee at Starbucks."

Kaparov took a sip, marveling at the taste. "No wonder you spend money on this."

"Well, I don't have a two-bottle-a-night vodka problem to feed," said the agent.

"Touché," said Kaparov, raising the cup.

They both stifled laughs, settling into their chairs. Prerovsky finally picked up the coffee, opening the top and taking a long drink.

"I have to brief the deputy director in ten. What's going on?" said the agent.

"Reznikov surfaced," said Kaparov.

"That sounds like a problem for the Bioweapons and Chemical Threat Assessment Division. Not organized crime," said Prerovsky.

"Actually, it falls under both," said Kaparov. "He showed up at a resort in Uruguay with Valery Zuyev."

"With Zuyev?" said Prerovsky. "Are you sure?"

"One hundred percent," said Kaparov.

"Shit. I'll need to brief the boss on this," said Prerovsky.

"You can't," said Kaparov. "Reznikov is dead. Remember? The SVR confirmed his death several months ago."

"This changes things," said the agent. "I'm sure the SVR could use this intelligence. Surely, Deputy Director Namakov has contacts in the foreign intelligence service that could put this to good use. Under the radar, so to speak."

"Yuri, when the SVR declares a scientist formerly employed by a supposedly nonexistent and highly illegal state-run bioweapons program to be dead—it's not a healthy idea to present evidence to the contrary," said Kaparov.

Prerovsky grimaced, shaking his head slowly. "We have to do something."

"That's why I'm here," said Kaparov.

"I'm not sure how I can help," said Prerovsky. "I'm one of six assistant deputy directors, and the most junior one at that. I basically run errands for the other five."

"That's what I hoped. No offense," said Kaparov. "They won't notice if you gather some information."

"Depends on the information," said Prerovsky. "The Solntsevskaya crew is well connected, if you know what I mean. Information is guarded."

"This shouldn't be a problem. We're talking about South America, not Russia or Europe," said Kaparov.

Prerovsky rubbed his chin, pondering the idea for several seconds before nodding.

"Zuyev in South America? I can work with that. The Chechens run most of the mafiya show down there, but the Bratva has been making some inroads. Bloody inroads. They're pushing into the Chechen-dominated European cocaine trade, which starts in the Andes Mountain region. It's not one of their well-established income bases, so I could dig around without drawing too much attention. What am I looking for?"

"He survived a messy assassination attempt in Uruguay. Near Montevideo," started Kaparov.

"Assassination?" said Prerovsky, taking a sip and staring at Kaparov over the cup.

"Americans," said Kaparov. "The same group that grabbed him before. They figure the Bratva will hide him nearby. They're looking for possible safe house locations."

"In that case, I'll take care of this myself," said Prerovsky. "I presume the Solntsevskaya Bratva will experience a significant setback in South America—and that will attract attention."

"Cover your tracks well, Yuri," said Kaparov. "The loss of Reznikov represents more than a setback for the Bratva."

"That's the only reason I haven't kicked you out of my office," said Prerovsky. "The thought of Reznikov working with the mafiya is terrifying."

"It wasn't the coffee?" said Kaparov.

Prerovsky stood up, extending a hand. "I have to get moving. I'll start digging into South America in an hour or so, after my morning briefings. I should have something by midmorning."

"Perfect," said Kaparov, shaking his hand. "Oh, I almost forgot."

He reached inside his suit coat and withdrew a plastic card from the inner pocket.

"In case you get cold feet," said Kaparov, handing him the card.

"A Starbucks gift card," said Prerovsky. "Just the thing to keep my mind off a cold, dark cell in Siberia."

"Vodka works better," said Kaparov, opening the door to leave. "Just in case you wanted a tip from an old-timer."

Chapter 18

Yuri Prerovsky tilted the flat-screen monitor away from
the door and typed his password into the department's
data archive system. His presence in the system wouldn't
attract any undue attention, since he'd subtly trolled for
an assignment related to the Solntsevskaya Bratva during
the morning meeting with the rest of the assistant deputy
directors. He'd even managed to convince one of them to
send him an email reminder to contact the FSB liaison
officer assigned to the Russian Federation's Argentinian
embassy.

Zuyev's arrival in Buenos Aires several days ago had
been duly recorded and reported by Russian informants
in the city. Travel to South America was not unusual for
Zuyev, in light of his position within the Bratva—and the
organization's not so secret plans to take business from
the Chechens.

The Bratva kingpin typically vanished a day into his
visit, feigning a trip deep into northern Argentina. Once
he had completely eluded Chechen and federal law
enforcement surveillance efforts, he no doubt returned to
Buenos Aires to conduct business. It made sense for

Prerovsky to poke around the Solntsevskaya files before contacting the liaison officer.

He navigated to the neatly digitized files and quickly pulled up information regarding known safe houses. After scanning through several dozen entries, only two locations stood out. A heavily defended compound in a sketchy industrial zone on the western outskirts of Buenos Aires or a tight cluster of Bratva-owned apartment buildings, clubs and storefronts in a Russian-dominated neighborhood south of the city. He studied the intelligence collected for each place, quickly drawing a conclusion.

The Bratva-owned city block presented a costly nightmare for any attacker, but the same features that made it a death trap could ultimately be turned against the Russians. The area was too porous. The right unit, using the right tactics, could rapidly access the main building—where suppressed weapons, practiced tactics and expert marksmanship would dominate. Prerovsky shook his head. Too risky for a valuable asset like Reznikov.

The compound west of the city made the most sense. Long sight lines for spotting an incoming attack. Three hundred and sixty degrees of open space immediately surrounding the outer perimeter. One access point at a manned, retractable gate. Heavily defended. If Reznikov ended up in Buenos Aires, the Bratva would bring him here. Of course, he didn't think like a Bratva Avtoritet or a special operations planner, so maybe it would be prudent to let the beneficiaries of this information make the decision.

Prerovsky spent the next several minutes taking screenshots of the files and saving them directly to a thumb drive, which he'd deliver directly to Kaparov within the hour. Before he left his desk to make his usual rounds through the department, a "top priority" email hit his inbox. He read the flagged email, shaking his head.

"Looks like this might not matter either way," he muttered, pocketing the thumb drive.

Regardless of the email's obvious implications, he'd deliver the information. Better to let the interested parties sort it out.

Chapter 19

Jessica paced back and forth across the worn carpet, casting a glance at the satellite phone on the nicked dining room table. Dammit, Berg. How long could it take?

"He'll come through with the intel," said Melendez, wiping the sweat off his face with a dirty towel.

He sat in a chair leaning against a water-stained wall, his eyes drifting shut every few seconds.

She checked her watch. Almost five in the morning. Close to eleven o'clock in Moscow. This was taking too long. They'd been up all night anticipating a call. Sanderson promised he'd call as soon as Berg passed along the information. Movement in the French doors caught her attention; the thin white sheer panel parted to reveal Talia's face. The door handle moved next.

"I don't have anything to report yet!" said Jessica, annoyed with this bitch's insistence on checking every few minutes.

She hated feeling helpless, but there was nothing she could do at this point. The Mossad had Daniel, and they wouldn't release him until she delivered the information—assuming Berg's intel was good enough for them. And that was a big assumption. She didn't want to think about that scenario yet, because she was hot, exhausted and unlikely to come up with a plan that didn't involve gutting the woman opening the door.

"We're running out of time," said Talia, pushing the door open a crack. "The Russians won't stick around for long."

"I don't have any control over the flow of information," said Jessica. "And if you open that door any further, I'm going to knock your head in."

The door flew inward hard enough to break several panes of glass—revealing the presence of more Mossad agents. A brutal-looking, over-testosteroned man with a thick brow stepped over the broken glass.

"You're alive because we need information," said the operative.

Melendez had already left his seat, circling behind Jessica with a pistol he had retrieved from one of the safe house's hidden wall compartments.

"It's fine, Rico," said Jessica, surprised by her own rational approach. "They lost two of their own yesterday."

The man eyed her with murderous contempt. "You don't have to look your friend's murderer in the face. A mercenary's face."

"Only one person in this room has been paid to be here, and it's not me or my friend with the pistol," said Jessica.

The man's eyes darted to Melendez, who stepped into the light from the adjacent room, holding the pistol low.

"You know what I mean," growled the Mossad operative.

"Not really," said Jessica, turning to Talia. "Is your team going to be a problem moving forward?"

"You're not exactly winning them over with your warm personality," said Talia.

"I thought I was being downright friendly given the circumstances," said Jessica. "Did I somehow miss the part when you released our operative?"

"He's fine," said Talia.

"Yeah, he's in really good hands," said the man standing inside the doorway.

The satellite phone chimed, stopping her from making a threat. Jessica grabbed the phone off the table, without taking her eyes off the Mossad operatives, and pressed "connect."

"What's up?" she said.

"Looks like you've made some new friends," said General Sanderson. "Don't answer that. The less they know about our surveillance capabilities the better. I received the data package. Reznikov is being held in Buenos Aires. Tell them we'll transfer the information in exchange for our operative."

Jessica turned the mouthpiece away from her face. "Reznikov is in Buenos Aires. You get the data when we get our operative."

Talia ignored her, instead addressing an unseen Mossad agent in the other room. "Buenos Aires. Get everything moving in that direction."

Feet shuffled outside of the dining room as the

Mossad team responded.

"I'm going to assume you heard me," said Jessica.

"I heard you fine," said Talia. "We'll release your guy after a successful operation. Can't be too sure."

Jessica tensed, but before she could fire off an angry response, Sanderson's voice of reason spoke over the phone.

"Don't respond to that. Just nod and put me on speakerphone," he said. "And Jessica, I need you to go along with whatever I say or propose. I will not let you or Daniel down. Start nodding like you're agreeing with me."

She tightened her face and nodded, adding a little dramatic flair to Sanderson's instructions.

"Understood," said Jessica, pressing the speakerphone button. "He wants to talk to you."

Talia shrugged her shoulders. "We're not handing him over until the operation is finished."

Sanderson's voice filled the room. "I'm not going to bullshit any of you. What happened yesterday sucked for both of our organizations. Good people died because our respective agencies don't share critical intelligence. That's the bottom line—so get it out of your heads that the woman holding the phone murdered your friends. Fortunately, we both get a second shot at taking out the Russians. "

"*You* don't get a second shot," said Talia. "Our teams will handle the takedown."

"Fine. You release my operative, and the data file is yours," said Sanderson. "You can do whatever you want with the intelligence."

"We've been through this already," said Talia. "At the successful conclusion of the op, you'll get your man back."

"Frankly, I'm not optimistic about your chances of success without our help, which is why I'd prefer to get my operative back in advance," said Sanderson.

"I think you underestimate our capabilities," said Talia.

"I would never underestimate the Mossad," said Sanderson. "But after analyzing the target area data, I stand by my assessment. You either release my operative in exchange for the intelligence, or we plan and execute this mission together."

"We have more than enough people to carry out the attack," said Talia.

"You're going to need my operatives to get close to the safe house," said Sanderson. "We're talking about a full city block owned and operated by the Solntsevskaya Bratva—set in the middle of a predominantly ethnic Russian neighborhood. You don't exactly fit in," said Sanderson.

Jessica stifled a laugh. Sanderson was right. The Israeli strike team looked very—Israeli.

"We're not planning a gradual infiltration," said the Mossad operative standing next to Talia.

"The Bratva is at war with the Chechens for control of the Andean cocaine supply lines. I can almost guarantee an RPG up your ass if the plan involves SUVs with tinted windows," said Sanderson.

"How would you do it?" said Talia.

"Are we working together?" said Sanderson.

"Screw this guy," said the other Mossad agent. "He's running a South American mercenary shop. Some of us speak Russian."

"I guess it's disco ball time," said Sanderson.

Jessica reacted instantly, lowering the phone and burying her eyes in the crook of her elbow. Even with her eyeballs pressed into her arm, she could detect the Xenon strobe lights. Despite the safe house's dilapidated appearance, several expensive, high-tech modifications had been made to enhance its security. On top of a sophisticated audio and video surveillance system was the latest in nonlethal, light-pulse incapacitation systems.

Yelling and chaos erupted inside the house as feet scrambled and bodies toppled furniture. The noise settled moments later, replaced by swearing and angry threats. Russian voices bellowed throughout the house.

"You can open your eyes now," said Sanderson.

She lowered her arm and smirked. Talia and her mouthy companion were down on their knees, eyes squeezed shut, with suppressed AK-74 rifles pointed at their snarling faces. The men holding the rifles were dressed in neutral street clothes. Cargo pants, khaki or gray, with untucked, loose-fitting shirts. Dark tattoos ran the length of their exposed arms, disappearing under short sleeves and reappearing on their necks.

"They sold us out," said one of the Israelis.

"No, they didn't," stated Talia. "They're making a point. A rather brilliant point."

"I wouldn't say brilliant," answered Sanderson. "But my Russian Group operatives can tip the scales in your favor on this mission. I highly suggest you use them."

"All right," said Talia. "We can work with this."

"Stand down," said a familiar voice.

Jessica shook her head. "Not until they release Daniel."

The "Russians" lowered their weapons and stepped back, maintaining a ready posture.

"We'll get to that," said Richard Farrington, passing the open door to the cellar on his way from the kitchen to the dining room.

The team must have slipped into the basement during the night. Farrington winked at her as he entered the dining room. She interpreted the wink the only way she could under the circumstances. Play along.

PART THREE

ALWAYS BET ON BLACK

Chapter 20

Reznikov leaned his head against a thankfully odorless pillow and stared at the ceiling of his latest accommodation, marveling at the absence of a ceiling fan. Over the past year, the absence of this seemingly ubiquitous South American fixture meant one thing—stifling heat. No longer.

A rectangular air-conditioning unit mounted high on the wall of his room kept him pleasantly cool. He wished it was secured to a window, but Zuyev had insisted on a completely contained environment, for security reasons. A view would come later, along with an unlocked door, or so he was promised. At least they had gone to some lengths to make his temporary stay pleasant.

The space contained basic, yet comfortable modular furniture, resembling a college dorm. A separate, closable enclosure held a small washbasin and a toilet, another luxury that hadn't always been guaranteed during his exile to the "tri-border" region. A half refrigerator at the foot of his bed hummed, competing with the air conditioner. It came fully stocked with assorted jars of pickled fish, cheeses and other savories that he had requested.

Of course, the crown jewel of his "apartment" was the makeshift liquor cabinet above the small kitchen efficiency area. He'd sacrificed most of the kitchen storage space to accommodate this critical addition to his living space. If they meant to keep him sequestered until the danger passed, he intended to make the best of it—at least that had been his justification for demanding several hundred dollars' worth of premium booze.

The bottles rattled in the cabinet, drawing his attention. He was tempted to indulge, but his head throbbed, and the queasy nauseous feeling showed no sign of abating. It would all subside eventually, leaving him free to obey the dark masters clinking in the latched cabinet.

He needed them after yesterday. Needed them desperately. No matter how indifferent or cruel his Bratva captors could be, they paled in comparison to the American psychopaths. Flashes of Stockholm made him reconsider his decision.

"A drink or two to help me forget," he whispered, knowing the final drink tally would fall more in the bottle or two range.

Kaparov's voice of reason didn't counter the argument. In fact, that voice had long ago died—snuffed out by the same dangerous concentrations of heavy metals that erased nearly every trace of his humanity.

Chapter 21

Deep shadows blanketed the narrow street, rendering the Cyrillic graffiti mostly unreadable. They had entered "Little Moscow" a few blocks northeast, noticing a significant decline in property upkeep the further they walked. Rusted gates, broken windows covered by cheap iron bars, weeds growing through cracked concrete slabs. Subtle signs of urban decay punctuated by the obvious— several shuttered businesses. The neighborhood had an empty feeling. No doubt the result of the Bratva's power grab.

"I suggest you start cussing in Spanish. Maybe grab at Grisha's crotch a few times," said Jessica. "Keep it authentic."

Talia shook her head and muttered a few choice slurs in Spanish.

"I'll pass on the grab," said Talia, swatting the "Russian" operative's behind and cackling out loud in Portuguese before whispering, "Probably not working with much down there."

"Nice," whispered Grisha, grabbing Talia and pushing her up against a graffiti-covered concrete wall.

He pretended to kiss her neck, instead whispering instructions that every operative heard through their earpieces. They rapidly approached one of the Bratva's soft checkpoints, on the southeastern outskirts of the Solntsevskaya's urban stronghold. They'd gone as far as they could go in the neighborhood—without getting into a fight. Hopefully a silent, one-way fight. They needed to get closer before moving up the assault team.

Her small group drew little noticeable attention on the way in, the locals turning a blind eye to their arrival. The visible tattoos on Grisha and Vanya marked them as Bratva, ensuring zero street-level interference. The people glanced at them long enough to determine they weren't Chechens, but not a moment longer.

Grisha and Vanya had been picked for their lighter skin color and obvious Slavic features. Ash brown hair. Blue eyes. Thin lips. Nobody could mistake them for Chechen infiltrators, which got them this far. The disguise would actually work against them when they reached the checkpoint. The tattoos would raise questions, along with suspicions. It was up to her to get them past the first checkpoint.

"You ready?" said Grisha, grinding her against the wall.

"I hope you're enjoying this," said Talia, wrapping her arms around him and reaching up under his loose shirt.

"Part of the job," he said. "Take your time and do it right."

"You wish," she said.

Grisha turned her toward the Bratva soldier twenty

feet away as she slid a suppressed, compact pistol out of his hidden beltline and lowered it tight against the left side of her miniskirt.

"Done," she whispered.

Grisha pushed her back against the wall, keeping the pistol side turned away from the sentries. Talia's pulse quickened as he stepped back and laughed at her in Russian before continuing down the street. She walked behind and to the left of the operative, switching the pistol to her right hand to keep it out of sight.

In addition to the two men hidden in an upcoming porch alcove, another Bratva soldier sat on a dilapidated concrete stoop directly across the street. Jessica blocked his sight line to the pistol swap by walking next to her, speaking rapid Spanish and laughing. The American team moved naturally. She had to give them that much.

"Do we have clear shots?" said Grisha.

"Zulu One clear," she heard.

"Zulu Three clear."

"Zulu Two standing by to engage identified targets."

"Team is set," whispered Grisha through the microphone, picking up the pace. "Engage on my mark. Three, two, one—"

One of the Bratva soldiers emerged from the alcove, speaking Russian. She eased her grip on the pistol and shifted her left hand in front of her.

"Mark," he said.

Grisha quickly shifted left, clearing her line of fire. With a practiced combat efficiency, she pressed the trigger as the pistol's green tritium sights came into alignment. The first bullet caught the approaching guard in the face; his body dropping as she made a minor adjustment to her aim. The second Bratva soldier reacted to the pistol shot by leaning forward, out of the shadows cast by the alcove. The next bullet hit him in the middle of the forehead, exiting the back of his head and smacking loudly into the door behind him.

Movement across the street drew her attention in time to see a pair of feet fall into the thick stand of unkempt bushes behind the iron fence. A few branches cracked as the weight of the guard's lifeless body thumped to the ground.

"Zulu One, target down."

"Zulu Three, target down."

"Zulu Two, the street looks good, but we made a little noise on that one. Lines of sight are clear, but I wouldn't be surprised if someone investigated," said Yoshi, the Mossad sniper.

"Zulu One and Three, move up. Two, watch the line of sight to the three-story rooftop," said Grisha.

"I have two rooftop sentries in sight. You're clear until you turn the next corner," said Yoshi.

"Copy," said Grisha, nodding at Talia and the rest of the team. "We're moving up to their hard security line."

The hard security line represented the street perimeter protecting the Solntsevskaya-owned city block. The corner of Elizalde and Coronel Dorrego Avenue, which loomed less than a hundred feet away, formed the eastern corner of the block's rectangular shape. Their approach from the southeast along Coronel Dorrego Avenue avoided sightlines to the taller building in the Bratva citadel.

Once they rounded that corner, all bets were off. A sentry pretending to peruse the scant aisles in one of the corner bodegas could sound the alarm with a cell phone call, or a sniper hidden deep within a darkened window in the citadel could pin them down before they crossed the street. They were about to enter the Wild West, as the Americans might say—and she couldn't wait!

Chapter 22

Jessica glanced over her shoulder in time to see the Mossad sniper leap from one rooftop to the next. The dark shadow vanished after crossing the short gap between crowded buildings. She walked in front of the men with Talia, swaying and laughing like she'd consumed a few too many tequila shots. Grisha and Vanya followed closely behind, ready to hand them weapons when they reached the corner.

"Zulu One in position," said Melendez. "I have two street-level targets midway down Coronel Dorrego. They'll have to go before you break into the open."

"Copy," said Grisha. "Zulu Two, target the rooftop sentries on the objective building."

"This is Zulu Two. I'm glassing them," said the Mossad sniper.

"Three," said Grisha. "Cover street level and windows along Elizalde, directly in front of target building."

"Settling into position and scanning," said Gosha, one of the Black Flag group's most experienced combat snipers. "I'll move up to the corner of Elizalde and Coronel Dorrego when you make your move."

Jessica had no idea where Gosha had hidden. The deep shadows cast by the buildings lining the street concealed his position, rendering him virtually invisible to the unaided eye. The snipers didn't have the same problem. They wore retractable head-strap-mounted night-vision goggles when they weren't searching for targets through the thermal imaging scopes attached to their sniper rifles.

"Anything on Elizalde?" said Grisha.

"Thermal images directly across from the target complex," said Gosha. "Thermal reflections at the corner of Dorrego and Elizalde closest to you. I have a possible in the bodega visible from your position."

"Copy. I just saw a head peek around the corner," said Grisha. "Watch the bodega for now, but I need you focused on the target building entrance when we break into the open."

"Understood," said Gosha. "Make sure the team stays to the right when moving down Elizalde. I need a clear line of fire."

"We'll hug the buildings," said Grisha. "Assault teams, start your approach. One way or the other, we should have the front door open for you shortly."

The assault teams, comprised mainly of Mossad operatives, would arrive in two armored SUVs—deposited directly in front of the gated courtyard entrance to La Suena Colonia apartment complex on Elizalde. The apartment complex penetrated deep into the Bratva-controlled city block, serving as an urban headquarters for the gang. Two teams of six Mossad operatives would search room by room until they located Reznikov, under constant attack from the Bratva muscle housed inside.

Fortunately, the detailed intelligence provided by Berg suggested that a significant portion of the Solntsevskaya gang would be out of the hive, working to establish control of the more lucrative parts of Buenos Aires. With Sanderson's crew controlling the streets, the Mossad teams could focus on their close-quarters combat inside La Suena Colonia. Jessica didn't envy their job. Without a doubt, Talia's team would do the heavy lifting on the mission.

A shirtless, heavily tattooed Bratva soldier stepped onto the sidewalk in front of them, speaking in Russian. His partner remained hidden behind the brick corner, part of his leg exposed.

"Jessica goes shirtless," said Grisha. "Talia takes the other."

"That would distract everyone," said Melendez.

"I'm filing a harassment claim," whispered Jessica.

She moved her right hand to her side, edging it back along her thigh until Vanya pressed the hilt of her knife in her hand. Vanya yelled something in Russian, causing the tattooed Russian to laugh and the hidden Bratva sentry to step into the open. Grisha whispered, "Now," but she had already sprung into action.

Talia's bullet tore through the lurker's throat before Jessica had closed the gap to her prey, giving the Russian a fraction of a second warning. His right hand extended forward instinctively, responding to the sudden threat, and his left flashed behind his back.

She brushed past the outstretched hand, wrapping her left arm around the back of his head and yanking him into her knife. His body went limp, a pistol clattering to the sidewalk behind the lethal embrace as warm blood sprayed the brick wall next to her. She pulled him into the shadows a few feet from the corner on Elizalde, the knife still buried to the hilt in his neck.

"Beautifully done," said Grisha, reaching past her to help Talia move her lifeless prey.

He pinned the limp body against the wall and searched it for weapons.

"I'm not finding anything," he said, nodding at Vanya. "Check the corner for a weapons stash."

A snap overhead drew her attention to the street. A figure armed with an assault rifle stumbled out of the bodega's door, thudding to the pavement. His rifle slid to a noisy stop in the middle of the street.

"I saw one more guy in the bodega," said Gosha. "Civilian type. Unarmed."

"Armed with a cell phone," said Vanya. "We're on borrowed time."

"Ground, this is Zulu One," said Melendez. "Zulu Three's bodega shot turned some heads on Dorrego."

"Copy. Snipers, engage targets. We're ready to move," said Grisha, snatching a compact assault rifle out of Vanya's hands.

Jessica left the knife in the man's throat and rushed forward, accepting the second assault rifle Vanya found leaning up against the wall on the unobserved side of the corner. She pulled the AKS-74U's charging bolt back a few centimeters, checking for a chambered round. Seeing brass, she jammed the bolt forward, making sure to properly seat the ammunition. With her thumb, she moved the selector switch to semiautomatic.

Vanya heaved the weapon cache's grand prize over his shoulder—a loaded RPG-7.

"Say hello to my little friend," said Vanya.

"Knock it off," hissed Grisha, crouched against the corner.

The air above them cracked and buzzed as the team's snipers engaged visible targets. A muted crash sounded ahead, followed by dogs barking.

"Target building rooftop is clear," said the Mossad sniper. "I might have dropped one off the roof."

"Dorrego to your right is clear at street level," said Melendez.

"We're moving," said Grisha, running into the street with his rifle held low.

Jessica followed him, scanning left as they crossed in a diamond formation. Yelling echoed in front of them.

"Guards across Elizalde are scrambling," said Gosha. "Going hot."

Bullets from Gosha's rifle snapped to their left as they sprinted for the opposite corner. Several figures piled into the street in front of the target building, firing their rifles on full automatic. She centered the red dot in her rifle's sight on a long burst of automatic fire and pressed the trigger twice, repeating the process two more times—until bullets started to ricochet off the sidewalk around her.

"Let me do the work," said Gosha in her earpiece. "I'll tell you when to move forward."

"Three armed men on Dorrego," said Melendez. "Might need an assist."

"Got it," said Jessica, shifting her aim ninety degrees to the right.

Three figures dashed across the street, headed for a series of porches and alcoves built into the face of a long, three-story building. The last one carried a rocket launcher. The lead runner face-planted in the middle of the street, toppled by one of Melendez's bullets. Jessica fired a hasty string of shots at the two remaining Russians, striking one in the leg and causing him to tumble. She tracked the rolling shadow through the red dot sight, repeatedly pressing the trigger until it stopped moving. The third Russian reached the safety of a low porch, reemerging with the RPG. His head snapped back as a suppressed snap echoed above.

"No offense, Jess, but rifles aren't your strong suit," said Melendez. "That was too close."

"Trade you," said Talia, extending her pistol.

Jessica begrudgingly swapped weapons, settling in next to Grisha.

"Are we moving yet?" she said, taking a peek and getting a face full of cement dust.

"One of them found a nice hiding spot," said Grisha.

"Not for long," muttered the Mossad sniper.

A single supersonic crack echoed overhead.

"Clear to advance," said the Israeli.

"Rifles up," said Grisha, rounding the corner.

Talia took up a position to his left, scanning the street ahead of them with her rifle, while Jessica and Vanya covered the sectors behind them. Gosha emerged from a thick stand of bushes a few hundred feet beyond the intersection and sprinted to his new position on the street corner next to the two dead Russians. He disappeared into the shadows, resuming his protective watch over their approach.

"Zulu Three in final overwatch position," said Gosha. "It's awfully quiet."

"Too quiet," said Grisha.

Gunfire erupted from the windows above the apartment complex's gated entrance, forcing her team flat against the building while bullets struck the curb and outer sidewalk—unable to reach them because of the steep angle. When the Bratva soldiers started to lean out of the windows to get a better shot, Grisha and Talia systematically cut them down with short, controlled bursts.

"RPG!" yelled Talia, firing her rifle at an open window directly across the street.

Vanya reacted swiftly, pointing his rocket launcher at the base of the window. The RPG's booster charge jolted the group, the chemical back blast instantly enveloping them in a thick, noxious cloud. A fraction of a second later, the rocket's booster motor kicked in, propelling the 93mm warhead through the brick wall on the other side of the street. The explosion knocked her team to the sidewalk, showering them with building fragments and wood.

Jessica crouched in the debris, helping Talia onto her feet, when a set of window shutters directly above them burst open. Jessica aimed the pistol at the opening and waited, firing two bullets when the Russian peered over the windowsill. In the darkness, she couldn't tell if her shots connected. Another set of shutters crashed open one story higher, knocking one of the wooden pieces into the street. Jessica shifted her aim as a rifle barrel poked through the dark window—followed by the shooter's full torso. Jessica and Vanya unloaded on the gunman with pistols, knocking him back into the room without his rifle, which bounced off the brick wall and landed in the street. Jessica started toward the rifle, but was stopped by Vanya.

"I can make an AK sing," he said, dashing into the street.

A coordinated string of street-level gunfire tore into the operative before he reached the rifle, flattening him next to the curb.

"Cover me!" screamed Jessica.

Bullets snapped by her head and bit into the street as she dragged Vanya with one hand and fired her pistol at the source of gunfire with the other. She reached the curb and tossed the pistol aside, grabbing him with two hands to pull him over the concrete lip. A sharp pain creased her right forearm, causing her to release her grip. She twisted her body and hauled him the rest of the way with her good hand as Grisha and Talia emptied their rifles at the unseen threat.

"Assault team, pull through the intersection of

Elizalde and Dorrego. Put your vehicles between the breach group and the primary target building access point. We're stalled out here and running low on ammunition. Dismount the vehicles on passenger side and prepare for a forced entry of the complex," said Grisha, tossing his rifle against the wall.

"Understood. Turning onto Elizalde now. Twenty seconds out," said the assault team leader.

As tires screeched in the distance, two men darted out of the courtyard entrance, firing on full automatic. Grisha's pistol answered the apparent suicide attack, striking each attacker multiple times—but the Russians continued to advance. Body armor.

Grisha adjusted his aim, hitting the closest Russian in the side of the head and knocking him backward into the second shooter. The momentary reprieve gave Gosha enough time to line up a shot with his sniper rifle, which passed between Jessica and Grisha and struck the second Russian in the chest. The man dropped to the uneven sidewalk, his fate far from conclusive thanks to the body armor.

Without warning, a long, fully automatic burst lit their faces, sprinkling them in hot shell casings. The body-armor-encased bodies twitched and jerked in place as Talia emptied the window shooter's AK-74.

"Just to be sure," said Talia, crouching next to them.

Grisha shook his head, continuing to search Vanya. "I don't know which one of you is crazier."

"She's a definite contender," said Jessica.

Chapter 23

The cramped SUV accelerated down Elizalde Boulevard, oblivious to the hollow thunks peppering the roof and sides. The thick tinted window next to Richard Farrington spider-cracked from a high-velocity bullet impact, obscuring his limited view from the rear compartment. Moments later, the vehicle jumped the curb and screeched to a stop on the sidewalk, disgorging the heavily armed, night-vision-equipped Mossad team through the passenger-side doors.

Farrington opened the SUV's rear barn doors, hopping onto the street as the gunfire intensified directly in front of the target building's gate courtyard entrance. The second SUV had continued down the street, stopping in front of the gate, its occupants sweeping the primary breach point with long bursts of automatic gunfire. Upon hitting the pavement, he turned to retrieve the oversized tactical duffel bag that had been stashed between Ilya and Farrington during the ride. Ilya, one of the team's newest members, pushed the heavy, compartmented bag forward where Farrington could reach it.

"Grab the rifles," said Farrington, pulling the bag out of the rear compartment and lumbering toward Grisha's team.

The Israelis had already stacked up along the passenger side, preparing to move forward. The female Mossad operative scrambled to don an array of tactical gear provided by her teammates. He was glad to see she was going in with the rest of the Israelis. Her absence on the street would make his job easier.

"Kit up. We have work to do," said Farrington, dropping the bag next to Grisha's team. "I'll take care of Vanya."

Vanya's situation didn't look hopeful. Lying on his back in a widening pool of blood, the operative was barely conscious. Farrington counted three wounds, at least one of them a jagged exit point. He unzipped a pouch on the side of the bag and removed a field trauma kit while the others raided the main compartments for night-vision gear, tactical vests and helmets. His first priority was to stop the bleeding.

"He needs more than a sprinkle of Celox and a plasma drip," said Jessica.

"Focus on your jobs," said Farrington, unraveling the medical kit. "NVGs first. The lights are about to go out."

Talia gave an order to the Mossad team, putting them on immediate standby to move out. She lowered her helmet-mounted NVGs and called out to Farrington.

"We're going in," she said. "Kill the lights and set up your perimeter."

"Not until you release our operative," said Jessica,

132

moving toward Talia.

"That was the deal," added Farrington, sprinkling a packet of blood-clotting powder over Vanya's various wounds.

"You'll get your guy back when we have Reznikov. That's the deal now," said Talia.

Before Farrington could intervene, Jessica lunged at Talia, yanking the pistol out of the Mossad operative's vest and jamming it under her neck. Within a fraction of a second, two rifle barrels pressed against Jessica's head; the rest of the Mossad teams' weapons were trained on Farrington's crew.

"Jess," said Farrington, "trust me. Let it go. I get the distinct impression that these people don't fail—at anything. Let them do their job, and we'll get our guy back."

He watched her closely, hoping she could process the situation. Killing the Mossad agent ensured everyone's death, including Daniel's. Accepting the sudden change to the deal kept the team alive, and gave Daniel a fighting chance.

She lowered the pistol, stuffing it into Talia's holster. "Next time I pull the trigger."

Talia pushed her away. "Kill the power."

"Right away," he said, switching tactical frequencies on his vest-mounted Motorola. "Support, blow the transformers."

"Copy that," said Gupta, from a hidden location several blocks away.

Seconds later, three successive explosions echoed over

the gunfire, killing the streetlights and darkening the surrounding buildings. Inside the courtyard, shooting gave way to panicked yelling as the two Mossad teams breached the gate and started methodically killing Bratva soldiers in the dark.

"We should load Vanya in the back," said Jessica, strapping a pair of night-vision goggles to her head.

Farrington stood up and reached behind her, his hand fumbling with the back of her miniskirt. For a moment, Jessica thought he had lost his mind. Before she could knee him in the groin, he ripped the cigarette-pack-sized wireless radio transmitter out of her back pocket and switched it off. The rest of the team did the same. He tossed the transmitter on the ground next to Vanya's and stomped on them.

"He's not leaving in one of these vehicles," said Farrington. "And we're not setting up a perimeter."

The sound of approaching vehicles filled the street as the gunfire drifted further into the courtyard.

"What the fuck, Rich?" she hissed. "They'll kill him if we bail."

Farrington didn't have time to explain the situation on the street. He needed one hundred percent focus until they had safely escaped Little Russia. They still faced a formidable enemy, and mission failure came in all sizes, small and large.

"Daniel is in no danger. Sanderson has personally taken care of the situation," said Farrington, handing her a loaded M4 rifle and two spare thirty-round magazines. "I'll explain when we're safe."

Farrington lowered his NVGs, taking in the bright green image provided by the rapidly approaching infrared headlights. Flashes exploded above them from the highest windows as desperate Bratva gunmen sprayed the arriving vehicles.

"Deploy smoke," he said. "Snipers get ready for pickup."

While he taped thick compresses to Vanya's bullet wounds, Grisha and Ilya threw cylindrical canisters in both directions, heaving a few as far as the intersection. The smoke grenades popped, billowing thick clouds of smoke that rapidly filled the street. When the two armored Suburbans pulled alongside the team several seconds later, visibility was close to nonexistent.

Farrington loaded Vanya into the back of the first vehicle, pulling Jessica inside before pulling the rear doors shut.

"Let's go!" he yelled, bracing for the sudden departure.

The SUV raced forward, briefly stopping at the edge of the smoke screen to pick up Melendez and Gosha. The vehicle slowed a few blocks later, turning onto a fully lit boulevard lined with active shops and restaurants. He handed a bag of plasma to Jessica and ripped Vanya's right sleeve near the crook of his elbow.

"Keep us steady," said Farrington, concentrating on the placement of the IV catheter needle in Vanya's arm.

"What's going on, Rich?" said Jessica. "This doesn't look like something you threw together at the last minute."

"Reznikov is gone," said Farrington. "Hold that up higher, please."

"Rich, I'm fucking tired and agitated—a really bad combo for me," she said, holding the bag against the rear compartment's roof. "What the fuck is going on?"

"The intel Karl Berg passed along indicated that Zuyev had departed Buenos Aires yesterday evening. No method listed, just 'high confidence' in his departure. Given the circumstances, we assumed that Reznikov travelled with Zuyev. They were gone before we received the intel."

Jessica shook her head. "Then what the hell were we doing back there?"

"Saving Daniel," said Farrington.

Chapter 24

Talia pulled the pin on a round fragmentation grenade and lobbed it down the hallway, landing it between two doors occupied by Bratva soldiers. She fired a quick burst at the gunmen to dissuade them from throwing it back, and ducked inside the stairwell landing. The walls and floor shook from the blast, fragments peppering the door frame next to her. A wave of burnt embers and thick smoke billowed past as she burst into the dark corridor with her team. She passed a set of closed doors and stopped, focusing her infrared laser between the scorched, open doorways ahead.

The operatives behind her simultaneously breached the closed doors, blasting the doorknobs with shotguns. Her previously crisp green night vision had turned hazy from the smoke, the unavoidable side effect of using grenades indoors. She preferred not to use them, but they didn't have time to engage in protracted gun battles on each floor. They were already pushing the outer edge of their time limit. A police response was inevitable with this much gunfire, even with the Americans messing with the police frequencies.

A head peeked through the doorway on the right, followed by a rifle muzzle. Talia centered the green infrared laser on the head and fired twice, staining the door frame dark green.

"Left clear," she heard in her earpiece.

"Right clear."

They moved up to the next set of scorched doors and threw flashbangs inside, repeating the room-clearing process. Both shooters were already dead. One from Talia's bullets. The other from her fragmentation grenade.

"Assault Two, what is your status?" she said, waiting for the team clearing the other wing to report.

A few moments later, Assault Two responded.

"We're getting close to the last hallway. Same pattern. Two out of three rooms are empty," said the commando. "They should have more people inside."

She agreed. Resistance had been fierce on the outside, but once her team breached the gate, the numbers didn't add up. Intelligence suggested that part of the Bratva garrison would be absent, not most of it.

"Copy that. Keep looking," she said. "Ground, this is Assault One. What is your status?"

"Perimeter is secure," said the garbled voice. "No police response, yet."

She stopped between the open doors. Police sirens blared nearby.

"Ground, I'm hearing police sirens," said Talia.

"Ummm. Yeah, we hear them too, but they're pretty far away," said the voice, in what she could swear was a light Indian accent.

"Zulu Two, this is Assault One. What are you seeing and hearing on the ground?" she said, getting no response from the Mossad sniper.

"Any unit, respond," she said.

"This is Assault Two. The sirens sound really close," said the commando.

"Can you see our vehicles from your position?" demanded Talia.

"Stand by," said Assault Two.

One of the team's operatives crouched next to her, pointing a shotgun down the hallway.

"This is taking too long," said Avi. "Where the hell is Reznikov—or any of the high-level mafiya?"

She was starting to get a bad feeling about the operation. Even if the voice hadn't been Indian, it didn't sound anything like the American operative in charge of ground security.

"Assault One, this is Assault Two. The vehicles are still there, but that's about all I can see. I think we started a fire on the ground floor. Elizalde is filled with smoke," said the other team leader.

"We didn't start a fire," said Talia, stepping into the room facing Coronel Dorrego Avenue.

She smelled it before she reached the window. Chemical smoke.

"Assault Two, abort the mission," she stated. "Ditch your radios and switch to secure cell phones. Assemble in the courtyard immediately."

Talia removed her wireless transmitter and turned it off, stuffing it in one of her cargo pockets. When she emerged from the room, each team member had done the same.

"What now?" said Avi.

"We move directly to the courtyard and assess the police situation," said Talia, "while I make a phone call."

She formed up in the middle of the group and unzipped the pouch on her vest containing an encrypted satellite phone, dialing the number to a newly established Mossad safe house in the slums of Montevideo. The call connected after a long wait.

"Terminate the American," she said, before anyone answered.

"Is that any way to treat allies that give more than two billion dollars a year in military aid to the Jewish state?" said a voice she distinctly remembered from earlier that day.

It sounded a lot like that pretentious asshole in charge of the Americans. General Sanderson. Former general. David had warned her not to trust him—but he gave her no indication that he wasn't fully committed to finding Reznikov. She should have listened.

"What did you do to my operatives?" she demanded.

"They'll be fine," he said. "And I don't mean *fine* in the Mossad interpretation of the word."

"Reznikov was never here, was he?" she said, following her team down the stairwell.

"Intelligence indicated that he left Argentina last night," said Sanderson.

"So you abandon my team in the middle of the most dangerous city block in Buenos Aires?" said Talia. "I don't get it."

"I needed to keep you occupied until I recovered my operative," said Sanderson. "It took a lot longer than expected to find him."

The door below them burst open, emptying two armed men onto the second-floor landing. Bright green muzzle flashes illuminated the stairwell walls, and the Russians dropped into a tangled heap.

"It sounds like you're busy. I'd love to continue this conversation later," said Sanderson.

"You better hope we get out of here. All of us," said Talia.

"I have little doubt you'll safely navigate your way out of this mess. I left you a duffel bag filled with smoke grenades next to the vehicle on the sidewalk. I trust you'll put them to good use. I recommend taking Coronel Dorrego Boulevard south. Police have already set up vehicle barricades a few blocks north," said Sanderson. "And, Neta?"

She froze on the stairs. Neta Brin's team didn't even know her real name.

"Yes?" she said, expecting a threat.

"Don't forget your sniper," said Sanderson. "You can talk to him on the tactical net again."

"I won't forget," said Talia, disconnecting the call before muttering under her breath.

"Any of this."

Chapter 25

The thick metal access door squealed, but he barely had the energy, or the will, to take his head out of the toilet bowl to see who had entered the room. He managed to lift his head a few inches, blurry vision adjusting to the watch in his face. Crusted vomit covered most of the watch face, a reminder of his wretched condition. Not that he needed one. Despite the thick yellowish film, he managed to determine what he suspected. This wasn't one of his regularly scheduled meal times.

"Damn it!" a gruff Russian voice yelled into the room. "We gave you a toilet and buckets for a reason."

Zuyev? He hadn't seen that asshole since they arrived at the dock. Reznikov pushed against the dirty plastic toilet seat with his arms, hoping to gain enough leverage to separate himself from the stained bowl. He teetered backward, coming to rest against the rattling wall. Zuyev appeared in the doorway and shook his head with a look of disgust.

"I would have put the 'Please Clean My Room' sign on the door handle," said Reznikov, "but someone locked my room—from the outside!"

"Security precaution," said Zuyev.

"It's been forty-eight hours!" said Reznikov, suddenly feeling energized.

"I like to be conservative with the protection of my most valuable investments," said Zuyev. "Especially in light of what happened at the resort."

"We got lucky at the resort," said Reznikov.

Zuyev eyed him curiously.

"Two of their people were dead before we left the room!" spat Reznikov.

"I thought you were too drunk to notice that," said Zuyev.

"I miss nothing," said Reznikov. "Even when I can barely see straight! Next time they will not botch the job."

"There won't be a next time," said Zuyev.

"You don't know these people," said Reznikov, rising from his crumpled position on the bathroom floor. "Killing me is their number one priority!"

"We're taking you where nobody would think of looking," said Zuyev. "Somewhere you'll be perfectly safe."

"Something tells me I don't want to hear the rest," said Reznikov.

"We can let it be a surprise," said Zuyev.

"No," said Reznikov. "I've had enough surprises for a lifetime. Where are we going?"

"Back to Russia," said Zuyev.

Reznikov's knees buckled, his sudden descent arrested by Zuyev's sturdy hands.

"Easy, my friend," said the Bratva commander,

bracing him against the bulkhead. "You look green."

"You're hilarious," said Reznikov. "I need a drink."

"The last thing you need is a drink," said Zuyev, motioning toward the empty bottles protruding from the sink.

"Vodka makes the crazy voices go away," he said. "And I just heard the craziest voice so far. It said I was going back to Russia."

"Russia was the highest bidder," said Zuyev.

Reznikov squinted, wondering if he was still asleep with his head in the toilet. Russia? Shit. No doubt he was headed to the Black Dolphin. Nobody escaped from that place.

"Prison," said Reznikov. "I should have known."

"Prison?" said Zuyev. "You've lost all sense of optimism."

"A year spent in the jungle sleeping with cockroaches will do that to a man," said Reznikov, now slightly hopeful that he wasn't headed to a maximum-security prison.

"Point taken. It's been a long year for all of us," he said, nodding at his bodyguard. "But now we move on."

The massive Bratva beast opened the liquor cabinet and removed an unopened bottle of Russian Standard. Reznikov watched the man's freakishly large fingers twist the top. He flicked the cap into the sink, bouncing it off the bottles onto the counter.

"Glasses, please," said Zuyev. "We're celebrating."

"What are we celebrating?" said Reznikov.

"Your appointment as director," said Zuyev.

"Director of what?"

"A joint venture that will make us all very wealthy. Come. This is not an appropriate place for a toast," said Zuyev, pulling him out of the bathroom.

Still dizzy from his perpetual state of nausea and intoxication, he allowed Zuyev to guide him toward the steel hatch near the front of the soiled and littered room. Reznikov had spent several hours retching in bed, unable to stand or even crawl his way to the bathroom—until the booze ran dry. While leaning against the kitchen counter during his first resupply run last night, he eyed the bathroom, somehow making the lucid decision to forego his urine- and vomit-soaked bed. He hoped to never see this room again.

A wave of humid air surged through the hatch, making him reconsider leaving the air-conditioned sanctuary. He could handle the filth. Heat was another story. They emerged on a metal platform two stories above the main deck. The steel creaked and groaned from the ship's movement. A strong wind swept across the platform, making it difficult for Zuyev to urge him forward.

"Come on," yelled Zuyev, pulling him toward the starboard side of the vessel.

Reznikov stared at the black clouds in the distance, fighting the urge to look down at the rolling waves.

"This is far enough!" said Reznikov, grabbing the safety rail next to him.

"Don't you want to see the sunset?" said Zuyev. "The storm is moving in right on top of it. A spectacular sight."

"I don't give a rat's ass about sunsets," said Reznikov.

"Let's get the toast over with before we're blown overboard."

With glasses in hand, Zuyev's bodyguard poured them a full shot of the clear alcohol.

"To the Bratva," said Zuyev, raising his glass.

Reznikov lifted the glass to his mouth, nodding at the mafiya boss before downing the shot. "The Bratva."

The glasses were refilled within seconds, Zuyev leading another toast.

"To your new position as director," he said, downing the glass.

Reznikov hesitated. "Exactly what am I the director of?"

"Russia's new bioweapons program," said Zuyev, grinning. "Under the Bratva's direct supervision, of course."

"Of course," he said.

Reznikov considered throwing himself over the side of the platform, but quickly determined that the distance to the main deck wasn't far enough to ensure his death. Nothing spoiled his suicidal moods more than the uncertainty. With his luck, he'd end up paralyzed from the neck down, sipping alcohol through a straw. Instead of a questionable death, he settled for the shot of vodka, followed by another. A slow demise was better than a botched one.

"Full research facility?" said Reznikov.

"State of the art," said Zuyev.

"State funded?" probed Reznikov.

"Not officially. State protected."

"No doubt state denied," said Reznikov.

"You catch on fast, my friend. The program doesn't exist," said Zuyev. "Come. We have better accommodations for you. From now on—you are one of us."

Reznikov nodded uneasily, not exactly sure he liked the implications associated with Zuyev's statement. *One of us* sounded a lot like *one of ours*—forever—and he had big plans outside of the Solntsevskaya Bratva.

The End

If you're reading these in order, *OMEGA*, book five, is the next in the BLACK FLAGGED SERIES.

For VIP access to exclusive sneak peeks at my upcoming work, new release updates and deeply discounted books, join my newsletter here:

http://eepurl.com/G4_qj

Visit Steven's blog to learn more about current and future projects:

StevenKonkoly.com

About the Author

Steven graduated from the United States Naval Academy in 1993, receiving a bachelor of science in English literature. He served the next eight years on active duty, traveling the world as a naval officer assigned to various Navy and Marine Corps units. His extensive journey spanned the globe, including a two-year tour of duty in Japan and travel to more than twenty countries throughout Asia and the Middle East.

From enforcing United Nations sanctions against Iraq as a maritime boarding officer in the Arabian Gulf, to directing aircraft bombing runs and naval gunfire strikes as a Forward Air Controller (FAC) assigned to a specialized Marine Corps unit, Steven's "in-house" experience with a wide range of regular and elite military units brings a unique authenticity to his thrillers.

He lives with his family in central Indiana, where he still wakes up at "zero dark thirty" to write for most of the day. When "off duty," he spends as much time as possible outdoors or travelling with his family--and dog.

Made in the USA
Lexington, KY
25 March 2019